Sid stepped back off the narrow stairs to allow the other person to pass. For a moment there was only a faint swishing. She peered down to see who was coming.

Suddenly a cold shimmering nothing brushed past her, a presence more felt than seen. Then it was gone.

The stairs felt empty now. Without thought, Sid plummeted down them. Clutching her bookbag in both arms, she ran off the stage, up the corridor and burst through the outside door. . . .

Still shaking, she breathed deeply of the cool evening air. Hold it, Sidonie, she told herself. Maybe it's time you concentrated on algebra and geography instead of fancy costumes and plays about witchcraft. And anyway, even if the theater *is* haunted, think how lucky you are to have seen it.

But as she walked swiftly away, she did not feel very lucky.

WHEN THE NIGHT WIND HOWLS

Pamela F. Service

FAWCETT JUNIPER • NEW YORK

RLI: $\dfrac{\text{VL: Grades 6 \& up}}{\text{IL: Grades 7 \& up}}$

A Fawcett Juniper Book
Published by Ballantine Books
Copyright © 1987 by Pamela F. Service

Library of Congress Catalog Card Number: 86-10851

ISBN 0-449-70279-0

This edition published by arrangement with Atheneum Publishers, a division of The Scribner Book Companies, Inc.

Manufactured in the United States of America

First Ballantine Books Edition: July 1988
Second Printing: February 1989

CHAPTER

Sidonie screamed. The girls around her screamed. With their leader, Abby, they fearfully watched the rafter and the bird Abby saw perching there. The witch bird, the spirit bird, ready to tear its vengeance upon them.

The little hall rang with screams and with voices yelling; Judge Danforth and Mr. Proctor, whom Abby now accused of witching their friend Mary.

Slowly Abby stood up from the plank bench and stared, terrified, at the rafter. As one, Sidonie and the other girls did the same. Across the room, Mary screamed, "Abby, you mustn't!"

Gripped by her witched spirit, the other girls echoed her. "Abby, you mustn't!"

"I'm here, I'm here!" Mary protested.

"I'm here, I'm here!" they echoed hollowly.

Horrified, Danforth shouted, "Mary Warren, have you compacted with the Devil? Have you?"

"Never, never!"

"Never, never," came the girls' echo.

Back and forth, the accusations, the yelling, the bewitched echoes. With the others, Sidonie swayed and whimpered, following Abby's every lead. Hysteria mounted. Mary shouted her innocence. Then Abby screeched, pointing to the rafter.

"Look out! She's coming down!"

On cue, Sidonie screamed with the others. High piercing screams. They flung up their arms to shield their faces from the witch bird's claws.

Mary's will broke. Gasping, she tore herself away from Proctor. "Don't touch me! You're the Devil's man!"

"Praise God!" the girls sighed in unison. Another soul in Salem saved; another condemned.

Sobbing and shaking, Mary gasped out her story: how Proctor had bewitched her, making her sign the Devil's book. Sagging onto the benches, Sidonie and the other girls sobbed quietly until in righteous fury Judge Danforth ordered Proctor to jail to await his judgment.

The stage darkened, and the curtain fell.

Muffled beyond the curtain, the audience was applauding. In the semidarkness of the stage, Sid got up, trying not to stumble over parts of the set or other members of the cast.

Once offstage, she found she was shaking. The end of Act III was always the hardest. She had to really get into it, to feel the fear. She could almost see how group hysteria could happen, how girls in up-tight Puritan Salem could work themselves into following a leader and almost believing that those hated adults really were witches.

Sid shivered. Her costume was soaked with sweat, and her throat was raw from screaming. Tonight she'd let out all the stops, screaming from her throat not her diaphragm as she knew she should have. But it was the last night of *The Crucible*. Everyone was giving it their all.

There was still one more act, but the girls didn't appear in Act IV, not even snobbish Viola Nolton who played Abby. In the big communal dressing room, Viola and the other girls were already laughing and chattering about that night's cast party.

Sid didn't find dropping her stage character quite that easy. Besides, she thought, watching some of them fawn over Viola, no matter how long she lived in this new town, there were some people she didn't care to fit in with. She skirted the others, heading to the tables with their rows of lighted mirrors to take off her makeup.

Her mother, who played the part of Elizabeth Proctor, was already there, fading out her rouge with pale powder and adding more lines and shadows around her eyes. She had part of Act IV to do yet where she's supposedly been in jail for months.

Her mother looked up and smiled at Sid. "Good job tonight. The screaming chilled me to the bone."

"Thanks. Maybe someday I'll get a part with a few more lines."

"Well, don't hope for too many. I screwed up that bit in Act II again. If Byron hadn't noticed and come out with the right line instead of the one I fed him the cue for, we'd have jumped halfway through the scene." She stood and replaced her prim white apron with a soiled and wrinkled one.

"Yeah, Byron's always with it. He's the only one who hasn't jumped something in that yelling and screaming scene."

"He's wonderful, all right," Mrs. Guthrie said, running a hand through her blond hair, carefully disarranging it. "I'd better go and be doleful."

"Break a leg!" Sid called out the traditional theater good luck as her mother hurried toward the stage.

Then she sank onto a stool and swiveled around to face a mirror. Taking off the starched white cap, she unpinned her dark shoulder-length hair and scowled at the picture before her. Thirteen, nearly fourteen, and still flat as a board. Lank black hair, face too thin, eyes too big.

3

Resignedly, she scooped up a cool dollop of face cream and smearing it over forehead and cheeks, eased off the base, eyeshadow, liner, and rouge. Frowning, she dabbed a tissue at the greasy mess. She certainly wouldn't wear this stuff on the street. If she was meant to look pretty like her mother, she told herself stubbornly, her body would eventually get around to it. Then maybe she'd be cast in better parts. But until then it wouldn't help to look like a phony Barbie doll, the way Viola Nolton and her friends did.

But stage makeup was something different. Close up it made people look like clowns, but from the audience it made features readable despite distance and stagelights. And it was fun, part of the specialness of theater. Each time before a show, putting on a new face helped her slip into that other character.

She sighed, rubbing away more and more of the most recent character. She was sorry to see her go. Not that she really liked this sheeplike Puritan girl, but she did like the chance to step out of herself into someone else for a while.

And she loved theater. She'd never done any until after her parents' divorce, when she and her mother had moved here from Indianapolis, and her mother had suggested they join the theater group. Sid had been terrified. The divorce and the move had been bad enough. But Mrs. Guthrie had done some acting in college and thought this would help them get involved in their new community. And in this small southern Indiana town, they needed all the help they could get.

Now, Sid had to admit not only was acting fun, but she was good at it. It was something she could do; something more hers than anything she'd done before. Besides, being part of the acting company did get her a certain amount of attention at the new school. Schoolmates treated her with a little more specialness than they might have done. After all, she was an "actress," and schoolmates who went to the shows boasted that they had a "friend" in the cast.

Sid shot the greasy tissues into the trashcan, and got up to wash her hands. It was good to have an idea of what she wanted to do with her life. Having a future somehow made getting through the present easier. She walked to where she'd left her street clothes. Slipping from the long skirt and laced bodice into T-shirt and jeans, she reluctantly took the final step from the seventeenth to the twentieth century.

Around her the other girls were changing and chattering. "And *so*," Viola said dramatically as she unpinned her wavy red hair, "I told Kevin just exactly what Kathy had said about *him*."

"You did?" gasped a couple of the others.

"So what did he say?" one pressed.

"Well, he turned *positively* white as a sheet. And what *he* said about *Kathy* isn't fit for your innocent young ears."

The others squealed. Sid wandered off. Boring. All those girls wanted to talk about was boys, and beastly ones at that. This was the last night of a terrific show, and for all they cared, they might as well be in the locker room at school. She wanted to be with someone who understood, who cared about theater as much as she did.

She left the dressing room and headed up the darkened corridor. On the other side of the wall, she could hear Judge Danforth yelling at Reverend Parris. Her mother's big scene was coming up.

Nearly at the front lobby, she turned aside and strode through a door marked "no admittance." It was dark inside. Almost by feel, she climbed the steep metal stairs, which creaked under her weight.

She stepped into the cramped light booth. The face and curly blond hair of the room's other occupant were lit only by light from the distant stage and by glowing dials on the control board before him.

5

"Hi," the boy whispered, turning to her briefly. "Your mom's about to make her entrance. Think I'll give it more shadow spot tonight. Make it more ominous."

From their perch above and behind the audience, Sid looked out to the stage. The gold plaster cupids adorning the proscenium arch were lost in shadow. But the stage they framed was starkly lit, showing the grim walls and bars of the Salem prison.

Sid glanced down at Joel Griggins as he hunched on his swivel stool, hand hovering over a switch. His eyes were intent on the scene before him. Joel was fourteen, a little less than a year older than Sid. But already he was recognized as a lighting genius and now served as almost the entire light crew of the Marjorie Trimble Blake Memorial Theater.

He was a tall boy and gangly, with outsized feet. His parents were astonished and somewhat disappointed that basketball, the natural birthright of all tall male Hoosiers, held no interest for him. He was a good enough student, but his real love was theater—not acting but the behind-the-scenes technical things, especially lighting. And although she was not on friendly terms with most boys, Sid liked Joel—perhaps because he also took theater seriously.

The boy lowered his hand on a switch. The light upstage became slightly more intense, casting a stark shadow against the stone wall as accused witch Elizabeth Proctor entered with slow dignity.

Sid tingled inside. She was proud of her mother. Proud that she had made a place for them and shown everyone what a good actress she could be. This was the biggest part she'd had so far; and she was so good Sid always found herself crying at the end.

Now Judge Danforth, stern in Puritan black, pleaded with Elizabeth Proctor to urge her husband to confess to witchcraft and save his life. But she promised nothing.

Their marriage had held little love. Yet now she was proud of her husband, proud he refused to confess to a lie.

John Proctor was led in. For this scene Byron Vincenti had altered his appearance even more than Sid's mother. His eyes were shadowed, his cheeks hollow, and his back was scarred with lash marks. Slowly, Joel brought up the light behind the barred window to a predawn gray. Danforth handed Proctor a paper to sign: a confession that he worked for the Devil and a denunciation of others who did the same.

Proctor realized now how much he loved his wife, how much he wanted to live. Yes, he confessed, he worked for the Devil. But he would not accuse his friends. Subtly Joel focused the lights on Proctor and Danforth as the climax approached.

Danforth demanded, "Then explain to me, Mr. Proctor, why you will not . . ."

"Because I lie and sign myself to lies! Because I am not worth the dust on the feet of them that hang!"

Danforth turned on him, his lips tight with fury. "You will give me your honest confession in my hand, or I can not keep you from the rope! Which way do you go, Mister?"

A tense pause. Proctor lunged at him, grabbing the confession and tearing it to shreds.

"Man, you will hang! You can not . . ."

His voice cracking with tears, Proctor was suddenly calm. "I can. And that is your first miracle, that I can." He turned to his wife. "Now I do think I see some shred of goodness in John Proctor. Not enough to weave a banner with, but enough to keep it from such dogs."

Elizabeth Proctor ran to him and clung sobbing against his chest. Lowering his voice, he said, "Give them no tear. Show honor now, show a stony heart and sink them with it!" Lifting her face, he kissed her.

Furious, Danforth ordered Proctor hauled off to be hanged. Others begged Elizabeth to plead with her husband. But sinking to her knees, stage center, she cried, "He has his goodness now. God forbid I take it from him!"

In the booth, Joel flipped several switches, and light from the newly risen sun poured through the bars to fall on Elizabeth's proud tear-streaked face. Drums rattled offstage, and the curtain fell.

Below the little booth, the audience burst into applause. Sid raised a hand and smeared tears from her cheek. Beside her, Joel flipped up the houselights and leaned back. "They were good tonight. You all were."

Sid's voice was thick. "Just pulling out all the stops, I guess. Byron was overwhelming wasn't he? But then he always is."

"He certainly gets into his roles, all right."

"I know. He seems to live for the theater. I guess he just does that carpentry stuff around town to keep body and soul together." She turned and started down the stairs. "I'd better go join the others; some folks might be coming backstage. I'm glad they decided against a curtain call for this show, or I'd never have seen that scene."

Backstage, the cast was holding court with friends and relatives. Sid recognized a few classmates, and was particularly happy to see Becky Johansen among them. The little group congratulated her on the good job she'd done. Then most gravitated off toward other acquaintances in the cast, but Becky stayed.

"It was all so wonderful!" she bubbled. "And Byron Vincenti was *so* handsome in that costume. I wish I'd come to see this show earlier, then I'd have known to come again and again."

Sid smiled. Her friend Becky was the victim of a staggering crush. She watched Byron Vincenti with starry eyes whenever he was onstage, but was overcome with shyness when she saw him on the street.

Squeezing Sid's arm, Becky slipped off toward the edge of the stage hoping for a fleeting glimpse of her idol.

Sid looked around the crowd and briefly wished her dad had been here to see this, or any of her performances. But he was busy with his new wife and family. Impatiently she shook her head to clear it of pointless wishes. She should be concentrating on her own new life, as her mother was trying to do.

Just then Byron Vincenti left the stage and began pushing his way through the throng toward the dressing rooms. Sid could see Becky shyly standing back, just drinking in the sight of him. More assertive theatergoers attempted to congratulate the actor, but he ignored them. He was always a moody fellow, and his current mood was clearly not to respond to the public. As far as Sid knew, he had neither relatives nor any special friends in town, though he'd been there some eight years.

But Viola Nolton was not to be put off. Boldly sidling up to him, she asked. "Are you coming to the cast party, Byron?"

He wheeled on her with the same scornful gaze Proctor had used on Abby. "After an experience like tonight, how can you think of such frivolity?" Viola gaped after him as he stalked off.

Weird, Sid thought. He's still playing a stiff-necked Puritan. And last spring, at the party after *H.M.S. Pinafore*, he'd been the life of the party.

Her mother would be disappointed though, Sid knew. Not that Mrs. Guthrie was actively shopping around for a man, but it was clear that she found Byron rather attractive. Of course, all the women in the theater group did. And he was good-looking, Sid had to admit. Dark, Latin good looks like old-time matinee idols. Even his name was exciting. Still, Sid couldn't make up her mind if she liked him or not. Byron was a little odd.

The crowd began thinning. Those actors still in makeup and costumes went to take them off. The set would be dismantled later. But tonight Martha Hills, the props mistress, was scurrying around trying to collect her props. Some had to be returned tomorrow to the people and shops she'd borrowed them from.

Martha's eye fell on Sid. "Sidonie, dear, I can't seem to find the poppet—you know, the doll your mother's supposed to witch people with. Will you give the stage another look for me?"

"Sure, Mrs. Hills." Walking through the wide door, Sid stepped onto the now deserted stage. Here, the backstage noises were muffled by walls and curtains. What had seemed a sinister prison was now merely plywood platforms and canvas flats crudely painted to look like stones.

Sid looked around the stage for the missing poppet. Nothing. She checked under the chair and table. Then, crouching down to peer under the platforms, she caught a glimpse of blue gingham. Climbing onto the lowest platform, she reached into the gap between it and the next, and fumbled blindly until she touched the battered ragdoll.

As she pulled it out, she realized she was not alone on the stage. Someone was standing stage left, among the narrow black curtains that concealed the wings. It was someone in Puritan black, and it looked like Byron Vincenti.

Standing up, Sid decided to strike a tentative blow for her mother. She stepped off the platform, walked toward center stage then turned to the wings.

"Byron, why don't you come tonight? Mother is bringing that same cheese casserole and . . ."

No one was there. No one could have been there. People

10

can't sneak around a stage in those Puritan shoes. They clomp.

Suddenly the empty stage felt cold. The rows of scats stretching off like tombstones seemed dark and menacing. It was as though in a single moment the scene had changed, and a frightful new play was about to begin. Shivering, Sid hurried out to join the others, with the witch doll clutched tightly in her hand.

CHAPTER

The next day at school, Sid was tired but happy. The cast party at the Noltons' had been late and fun, and she'd gorged herself on her favorite clam dip. Everyone, feeling close as a family, had sat around talking about the play. They'd laughed over the flubs and near flubs, and crowded to see the pictures people had taken.

Sid had covered her eyes at one rehearsal snapshot that showed her on the courthouse bench with her head thrown back and her mouth open like a howling dog.

"Did I really look like that?" she squealed.

"No," her mother assured her. "That's a split-second shot. The final effect was terrific." Sid decided to believe her. She'd rather not find theatrical immortality in looking like the Hound of the Baskervilles.

When they'd had enough of discussing past plays, they'd turned to the rest of the season. The tryouts for Gilbert and Sullivan's *Ruddigore* would be held in three weeks. Months of rehearsals would lead to performances in February. After that they'd begin work on *The Devil and Daniel Webster* for the June slot. A fun season and a fun party.

But now, that party and one show were over. Trudging home from school under a gray autumn sky, Sid felt the usual post-performance letdown. She kicked moodily at piles of leaves, but they were too soggy to make a satisfying scatter.

She plodded up Poplar Street, the town's main thoroughfare, past the conbined post office/bait shop and then the little limestone church she and her mother attended every Sunday. They hadn't been that faithful in Indianapolis, but since coming here, Mrs. Guthrie had instituted regular church as part of their "fit into the community" campaign.

And since the new pastor, Rev. Dennis Aikens, had come six months ago, it hadn't been so bad. The old minister had been heavy on sin and damnation, but Rev. Aikens was more rooted in the twentieth century. Maybe that was part of the problems he was having. He appeared to be fitting into this small set-in-its-ways town even less well than Sid and her mother. The congregation seemed uncomfortable with a minister who talked more about social involvement than the wages of sin. Sid had heard grumblings to that effect from customers at her mother's antique shop. She supposed it was a sign that they themselves were becoming accepted, when the locals were willing to gossip in front of them.

As Sid passed in front of the chruch, Rev. Aikens himself stepped out of the side office. He waved at her as if he wanted to talk. She waited as he walked briskly toward her up the leaf-strewn path.

His mustache, she thought. Maybe people wouldn't think he looked so much like a big city lawyer if he shaved off his blond mustache. But she wouldn't suggest it. She liked mustaches. Her father had one, though not so big and bushy.

"Sidonie, I just wanted to say I saw you and your mother in *The Crucible* last Friday. I meant to tell you after church what a fine performance it was. Your mother's very talented. She had me in tears. And I wanted to jump up there and argue theology with that idiot minister, even though I knew he was only the druggist."

13

Sid beamed. "Thanks. It was a good show, wasn't it?" An idea struck her. "You know, the theater always needs more men. Why don't you try out for something yourself. We're doing a Gilbert and Sullivan next."

He exploded into a laugh. "I guess you can't be listening too closely on Sundays, or you'd know how terribly I sing."

"Well, a straight play, then."

"I hardly have the talent to compete with the likes of you two," he said affably. "But I promise to come see your next show."

They parted, heading in opposite directions along Poplar Street. Sid felt a little better. Rev. Aikens was a nice guy, for all that he was a minister. She passed the sign proclaiming "Marjorie Trimble Blake Memorial Theater, one block." Impulsively, she turned up the hill.

Last night, Evelyn Bidwell, the wardrobe mistress, had made a half-hearted plea for people to drop by this afternoon and help decide which costumes needed cleaning and which could be sorted and stored. Sid had time this afternoon. Why not? It was one way to make it all last a little longer.

As she approached the theater, Sid looked it over with possessive pride. Where most community theater groups had to make do with a converted barn or school gym, their group had a real theater building. Built of brick and stone in the 1880s, it had been the gift of Marjorie Trimble Blake. Mrs. Blake, a celebrated actress, had, upon retirement from the New York stage, returned to Indiana. There she brought culture to the provincials by building and endowing a theater. The amateur troop that continued to strut its stage was recruited from this and surrounding communities. And although dramatic talent varied, there was always enough exuberance to attract not only home folks but regular theatergoers from out of town.

Sid let herself in the side door they'd been told would be open. She heard voices and headed toward the costume loft taking her favorite shortcut up the spiral stairs at the back of the stage and along the catwalk.

The costume loft was narrow. With three of its walls composed of wire fencing, it ran the entire length of the top floor behind the stage. The only things higher were the tracks for lights and the battens for hanging backdrops.

Two harried women greeted Sid with cheers of relief and soon had her rehanging piles of clothes that had been pulled out in the preproduction frenzy. After a while one of the women left with the final load of costumes for the cleaners.

To make conversation, the remaining one, Evelyn Bidwell, asked Sid about school. But though she nodded appropriately, neither she nor Sid were very interested in the answers. Soon conversation lapsed as each contentedly concentrated on her own work.

Finally the woman stood up stiffly from where she'd been crouching by a box of patterns. "Sidonie, I have to go home and make dinner now."

"If you don't mind, Mrs. Bidwell, I'd like to stay a few minutes and finish reorganizing these hat shelves. They're an awful mess, and all the *Mikado* wigs are getting smashed at the bottom of this box." She kicked a large cardboard box where a bunch of black furry shapes lay like run-over animals.

"That, my dear, would be a real service. But don't stay so long you miss your own dinner. Just let yourself out by a door with a panic bar."

Sid looked up questioningly.

"The ones with the long bars that are always unlocked on the inside."

"Oh, right."

Soon Mrs. Bidwell was gone, and Sid was alone in one of her favorite places in the world, the costume loft of the

Blake Theater. The spot seemed somehow to capture the exciting essence of theater—the glitter of professional make-believe.

She left the hat shelves and moved to the costume rack, reverently running her hands over the silky kimonos for *The Mikado* and the slinky velvet evening gowns for 1930s mysteries. There were dirndles for *The Sound of Music*, grass skirts for *South Pacific*, and long dresses with bustles or hoops for any of a number of shows.

She was just trying on a beaded black cape when she thought she caught sight of someone down below. Mrs. Bidwell coming back? Guiltily she slipped off the cape, returning it to the hanger. Or maybe Martha Hills was back looking for some missing prop.

Sid stepped closer to the loft's wire wall and looked through the mesh to the stage below. Something gray seemed to be moving about, but it was so dark it was hard to tell. Possibly the janitor? But surely he would turn on the light. Maybe one of the cast secretly come back to relive the glory of being on the stage. But she didn't hear any lines being recited. In fact, she heard nothing at all. No foot-steps—nothing.

She squinted more closely, but the gray shape seemed to fade away into the curtains. Maybe there had been nothing there after all. Just odd shadows—like last night.

Returning to the hat shelves, she continued sorting. But an uneasiness kept pricking at her. Lots of theaters were supposed to be haunted, weren't they? It was even supposed to be good luck. Lucky Blake Theater.

She worked more and more quickly until she noticed she'd mixed a bunch of men's lace collars in with the bonnets. After forcing herself to stop, she took three deep breaths. There were no ghosts, she told herself. It's only that you're alone in this big, very old theater. And even if you did see a ghost, that would be *exciting*, not frightening. Isn't that what you've always told yourself?

16

She looked at her watch. Still, it really was time to go. Adding one last battered crown to the headgear on the top shelf, she grabbed up her schoolbag and walked with deliberate calm down the short flight of metal stairs from the loft.

Before stepping onto the catwalk that ran along the back of the stage, she scanned the stage below. It was empty, except for the few remaining bits of set. Nothing moved.

More confident now, she walked along the metal catwalk to the top of the spiral stairs. She'd just stepped onto the topmost one, when she sensed someone coming up the stairs from below. Mrs. Bidwell must have returned after all.

Sid stepped back off the narrow stairs to allow the other person to pass. For a moment there was only a faint swishing. She peered down to see who was coming.

Suddenly a cold shimmering nothing brushed past her, a presence more felt than seen. Then it was gone.

The stairs felt empty now. Without thought, Sid plummeted down them. Clutching her bookbag in both arms, she ran off the stage, up the corridor, and burst through the outside door. So that's why they call them panic bars, she thought giddily as the door thudded closed behind her.

Still shaking, she breathed deeply of the cool evening air. Hold it, Sidonie, she told herself. Maybe it's time you concentrated on algebra and geography instead of fancy costumes and plays about witchcraft. And anyway, even if the theater *is* haunted, think how lucky you are to have seen it.

But as she walked swiftly away, she did not feel very lucky.

CHAPTER

By the next day, Sid had fairly well convinced herself that the happenings at the theater had been imagination. After all, for several months she'd been immersing herself in a period when people believed in witches, ghosts, and a real Devil. That was bound to affect how her mind saw things.

Just the same, for the next few days she walked directly home after school and dutifully helped her mother in the shop. Unquestioning normality seemed very appealing. But by Friday, she was so sure she had the situation under full mental control, she decided to take the more interesting route home.

She turned off on the path that ran between the church and the little graveyard. It was a pretty place, one she could never imagine would inspire fear. When the new minister had first come, she'd been afraid he'd try to "tidy up" the sleepy little churchyard: maybe pull vines off the crumbling drystone wall or clear away the lacy weeds and reset tombstones that had toppled over. But he'd done none of that, and she was glad. Perhaps he found it as pleasant and peaceful there as she did.

Sometimes she liked to wander among the tombstones, some recent, some dating back nearly two centuries. She particularly liked the ones carved like dead trees with climbing vines and mushrooms and the sad little stone lambs that sat over children's graves. Reading the inscriptions, she mentally collected all the quaint old names people had in those days, names like Permelia and Relief. She wondered what those people had been like and how their lives had been.

But today she walked on past the churchyard, past Mrs. Clement's large, well-organized vegetable garden, and out onto the street that ran past the theater. She couldn't go in; she had no key. But she felt that maybe just walking by it would be like getting back on a horse that has thrown you.

The sunlight, with the crystal clarity of a November afternoon, cast a ruddy glow over the brick façade. It highlighted the limestone cornice and the bevy of carved cupids that arched over the main entrance.

Sid stood studying the cupids and the comedy and tragedy masks they held. Suddenly the door flew open. Joel Griggins burst out, then turned and slammed the double doors behind him.

He hadn't seen Sid. But she'd seen the look on his face, and it suggested something familiar. Hesitantly, she walked up behind him.

"Joel, you look like you've seen a ghost."

He yelped and spun around. Seeing her, he relaxed, slumping his tall frame against the door. "I have. Three of them."

Instantly the color rose in his normally pale face. He looked embarrassed that he'd confessed to anything so childish.

Hurriedly Sid stepped in. "Well, don't worry, you're not alone. I've seen some pretty creepy things in there, too. Tell me about it."

He pulled himself together in visible relief. "Sure, but let's walk." Briskly he headed down the street without glancing back at the theater.

19

"I know the whole thing sounds crazy, but I really did see it."

He gave Sid an awkward sideways glance. She nodded encouragement. Hesitantly, he continued. "I dropped by today to check on what we have in the way of gels and such. *Ruddigore*'s going to need pretty elaborate lighting. Also the swivel on one of the follow spots is wobbly, and I needed to do something about it."

He glanced at her again, then cleared his throat.

"So anyway, I was up there in the booth, and I thought I saw someone moving around on stage. It was dark down there, but the light from the booth lit things a little. Well, I figured it had to be one of us, no one else has keys. So as a joke, I thought I'd switch on one of the spots. You know—catch them like an escaped convict.

"So I did. The big spot on the wide scope. But there were three of them, not one. And . . . they weren't us."

"Who were they?"

"I don't know. They looked like people, but gray and sort of out of focus. They were moving around doing . . . I couldn't tell what, just sort of walking and moving. But with no noise—like silent movie characters or something.

"For a while they didn't seem to notice the light. Then suddenly they stopped and looked up at the booth . . . and one by one . . . they went out."

"Out the door?"

"No, just out. Out like candles. Snuff! They were gone!"

The two had stopped under a tall elm on the street corner. Despite the bright sun, Sid shivered. "Have . . . have you seen anything like that before?"

"Nothing like that! Oh, I guess there've been shadows and stuff, things that made me look twice maybe. But you said you've, uh, seen things too?"

She nodded, staring down at the sidewalk, at the ghostly patterns left by rain-dampened leaves. "A couple of times.

Things that were there . . . then weren't. And, and a cold something. I don't know what, just something. You're right, it does sound crazy."

To Sid's surprise, Joel put his hands on her shoulders and squeezed. "It sure does. And am I ever glad it was *you* standing out here when I came running out like a crazy guy. Anyone else would think I'd flipped out."

She looked up at him and grinned. "You're the old theater buff. Haunted theaters are supposed to be *good* luck, aren't they?"

"I guess, as long as the ghoulies don't drop chandeliers on people like the Phantom of the Opera did."

She jerked in alarm then frowned at him. "Cut that out. Anyway, the Phantom wasn't a ghost. He was a flesh-and-blood madman hanging around in the sewers under the opera house."

Joel laughed and started walking again. "I don't know about the sewers. I was just afraid there was a madman working in the light booth."

Once on Poplar Street, the two separated. Sid headed home. In the bright sunshine on the familiar street, she could feel her life falling comfortably back together. Sure there was something weird in the theater, but now she knew she had actually seen it and not dreamed it up out of something weird inside her. And even in seeing it, she wasn't alone.

Turning the corner at the gas station, the sight ahead was even more welcome than usual. Set back from the street under its two old cedars, stood the house that was home, shop, and historical landmark all in one.

Sid still remembered the first time she had seen the place. Her mother had always loved antiques, and some weekends they'd driven for miles into the country looking at little antique shops. Then one Sunday, maybe six months after the divorce, they'd stopped here. In chatting with the couple that owned the place, Mrs. Guthrie had learned they were thinking of selling and moving to a condominium in Evansville. She'd thought about it for a week, then drove back and offered to buy—house, business, and everything. It would give her a chance to start a new life in a new place.

Sid had held plenty of reservations about the move, but she soon found she didn't miss the city as much as she'd expected. And she liked the house. The front part was old, maybe 1820s. Big rooms with fireplaces opened off each side of the entry hall. These were now the antique shop. The two rooms above were Sid's and her mother's bedrooms. In Victorian times and later, additions had grown onto the back of the house and these were now their kitchen, bath, dining room and parlor. Despite its age and occasional leaks, the whole place was warm and homey.

Sid swung open the wrought-iron gate, and Fred, their honey-colored hound dog, dutifully got up from the grass and ambled over to her. Tail wagging, he let himself be patted than shuffled back to his patch of sun.

Fred had come with the house. The old couple had thought he wasn't meant for a condominium. And Fred did seem content with his new people. In fact, he seemed content with everything. Sid had never seen such a laid-back dog. He wasn't all that old, she knew, just mellow.

Ritually she followed Fred back to his lying down spot where he rolled over and presented his tummy for scratching. Well, at least he's a good watchdog, she thought as she rippled her fingers through the warm golden fur. He had an impressive bark. Unfortunately, he usually accompanied this with vigorous tail wagging; but maybe a burglar wouldn't see that in the dark.

Sid rocked back on her heels and thought about burglars sneaking around the place at night, and then suddenly remembered a letter she'd received from a friend in Indianapolis a few weeks after they'd moved here. Her friend had wondered how Sid could stand living in an old house full of antiques. Wasn't she afraid of burglars, or ghosts?

For burglars they had Fred, and Sid had dismissed the thought of ghosts. Now, however . . .

She looked up at the old brick house and closed her eyes as psychics do in movies, trying to pick up supernatural vibrations. Nothing. Besides, weren't dogs supposed to be sensitive to the supernatural? She'd certainly never seen Fred bristle at protoplasmic nothings.

No, dismiss haunted houses. But a haunted theater now . . . She tingled at the thought. Sitting in the autumn sunshine with several days between her and her own experience, what she and Joel had seen was more exciting than frightening.

Fred sighed resignedly as Sid got up and hurried into the house. She wanted to talk with her mother about it. She'd have to be careful, though. Adults seemed to feel obliged to doubt children in such matters. She'd keep it sort of abstract.

She flung open the front door, jangling its little brass bells. Dropping her schoolbag at the foot of the staircase, she turned right into the main room of the antique shop. Abruptly she stopped. Her mother, standing behind the cluttered counter, was talking with a customer, a tall dark-haired man. With almost arrogant slowness, the man turned around and looked at her. It was Byron Vincenti. Every inch of him still seemed to be playing John Proctor.

But her mother was her usual cheerful self, if a little more pink cheeked. "Hi, Sid. Good day at school?"

"All right."

"Good, good. There're some brownies in the kitchen."

"Thanks," Sid started turning then added. "Anything you want me to do around here?"

"Yes. There's a box in the other room—things I just bought from Mrs. McGuire. Mostly dishes and such. Could you unpack them and put them in that empty case with the green lining? I'll price them later."

"Sure." Sid turned away, nodding briefly at Byron, and hurried off to the kitchen. Once equipped with a plate of brownies and glass of milk, she returned to the front of the house and went into the other antique-filled room.

She'd agreed to help her mother in the shop whenever she could, and it was a duty she really didn't mind. She liked old stuff. Even everyday things seemed strange and mysterious if they were old enough. She liked to imagine the people who'd used them and all the things they'd done and thought about. Sometimes she got so attached to items, she hated to see them sold. Hardly a businesslike attitude, she realized. But then she had her eyes on a career in theater, not business.

She cleared a space for her snack on a table full of mustache cups and shaving mugs. Several closed cardboard boxes sat in the middle of an aisle. Kneeling by one, she folded back the lid and sighed. This was a lot she wouldn't bemoan selling. Fiesta Ware dishes.

She couldn't imagine why people collected the stuff. Bright garish colors; ugly squat shapes. Nothing to stimulate the least twinge of romantic speculation.

As she dutifully unwrapped the china, dust rising from the papers danced in the slanting rays of afternoon sun. From the other room she could hear voices rising and falling in pleasant conversation occasionally touched by her mother's feathery laugh. She frowned. It wasn't that she minded her mother being interested in men again, or even her considering another marriage. That was sure to happen eventually. It was Byron Vincenti that worried her.

As well as being handsome, of course, he sang beautifully and was a marvelous actor. But he wasn't much else besides. Theater seemed to be everything with him. Maybe she'd like him better if he had a stamp collection or something. He certainly could be witty and charming, and at times last year he'd been a lot of fun. But he could also be cold, haughty, even cruel. It actually seemed to vary with the parts he played. Maybe that's what made him such a good actor, completely getting into his roles. Yet, Sid hoped that wasn't an absolute requirement for acting. She loved theater passionately, but didn't want to go quite that far.

The bells above the front door jangled as their visitor left, and immediately Sid turned her thoughts from darkly handsome leading men to the subject that had sent her skidding into the other room in the first place. Ghosts. In a flash of inspiration it occurred to her that this might be the solution to another problem that she'd been dismissing most of the semester—the topic for her English term paper. She smiled triumphantly. Here was a way to bring the subject up in a manner adults could accept.

Sid unwrapped the last piece of china, stood up, and hurried into the other room. "Mom!"

Her mother turned toward her looking rather distraught. Sid guessed she was in some flutter over Byron. A change of subject was clearly in order.

"Mom, I have to do a paper for English on some bit of Indiana folklore. I'm supposed to do research and interview people and all, and I just got an idea."

Her mother composed her face into attention. "And what is this inspiraton?"

"Well, you know that often theaters are supposed to be haunted. And . . . and I've heard rumors that ours is too. It might make a good subject. Do you know anything about it?"

Her mother laughed. "Is this a real anthropological interview? Where is your tape recorder and notebook?"

Sid frowned. "Well, I could get my tape recorder, I

guess." She perked up. "Does that mean you have something really spooky to tell me?"

"No, I was just kidding. I haven't much to impart on that subject." She swiveled her stool, looking with a thoughtful blankness at a shelf of china figurines.

"I *have* heard a couple of people say they've seen some odd things. But you know how strung out people get before a show. Once I thought I saw something too, but I didn't."

Sid plunked herself down in a wicker rocker, after first moving it so it didn't rock back against an end table. She'd already broken one vase that way. "Tell me about it anyway."

"Well, there really isn't much to tell. I was alone in one of the upstairs dressing rooms. I think it was before the dress rehearsal for *Brigadoon*. I was concentrating on getting my hair pinned up, but I knew someone else had come into the room. I started to talk to her. No one answered, though I could feel someone was there. So I turned around, and I was completely alone in the room. It was kind of creepy, but I know I just imagined it."

"Mmmm. What about the other people you said saw things?"

"They'd kill me if I set you on them. It was just the same sort of things. Just silly imaginings. But you know . . ."

"Yes?"

"Well, I was just thinking. If the Blake Theater really is supposed to be haunted, I bet George Prow, the janitor, will know everything there is to know about it. He's lived in town all his life and has worked at the theater for years."

Sid jumped to her feet. The chair thumped back against the window sill, jangling a string of glass prisms and spinning rainbows around the room. "That's it. I'll interview George. And I'll do it right. Tape recorder, notebook, everything."

"Well, better call him first," her mother suggested,

turning back to the pile of antique valentines she was sorting. "He may not take kindly to being a specimen for anthropological study."

However, when Sid finally got up the nerve to phone him, George the janitor seemed willing, almost eager, to be interviewed. She guessed it made him feel important.

But as she walked to his house the next Tuesday after school, Sid was having second thoughts, Suppose George had never seen a ghost in the theater, or refused to talk about it? For this paper they were supposed to use interviews, but if George didn't add anything, where would she turn? Her mother's "experience" was pretty vague, and she was sure Joel wouldn't want his name used. He could be an "anonymous source" of course, but then she might be accused of making it all up.

There were probably a lot of easier topics she could have chosen, if her sole interest had been the paper itself. One of the girls was doing Johnny Appleseed. For an interview she was using her grandmother who was a native Hoosier all right, but whose knowledge of the subject seemed to be based entirely on the Walt Disney movie.

Sid sighed. Well, at least she'd get high marks for originality.

George's house was on the southern fringe of town, but with a town the size of this one, that wasn't very far. The cold autumn wind herded a pack of fallen leaves along the road before her. The leaves skipped and tumbled over the surface until the pavement gave way to gravel. Doggedly she continued up the road, jumping over ruts full of sodden leaves and rain from the night before.

At last she came to a rusty mailbox faintly marked with the right number. Behind the weather-worn fence, the garden rustled with dry weeds. An old maple towered over the house, its branches still clutching a few bright orange leaves that glowed like flames against the gray sky.

The house itself was tiny. Sid felt a thrill of academic recognition. This was the type of house her mother had pointed out as the "shotgun" style, so called because, one room wide and two deep, you could shoot a shotgun "clean through" it, in the back door and out the front. Importantly, Sid whipped out her notebook and made a note.

As soon as she stepped through the gate, a little white dog dashed around the corner of the house and exploded into sound. She was glad she hadn't brought Fred. Fred never got into fights with other dogs, but his laid-back indifference drove hyper dogs to frenzy.

The dog yapped, and Sid stopped halfway up the path until the door opened and old George stepped out onto the tiny front porch.

"Daisy, shut your trap! Don't worry, Miss Guthrie, that dog don't do nothing but bark. But come on in, I've got some coffee going." He looked at her a moment. "Hmm, maybe you're a bit young for that. Got some pop, though. You'd like that?"

"Yes, please." Sid looked down doubtfully at Daisy, who was smelling the cuffs of her jeans and talking in throaty little growls.

"Cut it out, I tell you!" The old man aimed a half-hearted kick at the dog, who deftly sidestepped it then happily followed her master into the house. Sid came after, looking with fascination around the crowded little room. Her host disappeared into the second room to get refreshments.

A lifetime's accumulation of things seemed thrown together without thought to "decor" of any sort. On faded flowery wallpaper, a beer company calender hung next to an old print of hunting dogs in a carved oak frame. Above them hung a picture of Jesus painted in vibrant colors on black velvet. A small TV shared a lace-covered table with vases studded in seashells and a beautiful stained-glass lamp.

Sid thought the place looked like a yard sale moved indoors. But there were some things she was sure her mother would itch to have in her shop. The lamp for one and probably the blue-and-white woven coverlet thrown over the couch. Just last week she'd been dragged to an auction where one like it had gone for $500.

George shuffled back balancing drinks and a plate of Twinkies. He kept the chipped mug of coffee for himself and eased the plate and a bottle of Coke onto a magazine-strewn table. Settling into a rocking chair, he pointed Sid to the couch, that portion not occupied by Daisy.

Gingerly she sat on the maybe priceless coverlet, then unslung the tape recorder from her shoulder and placed it on the table next to the Twinkies. She pressed the red "record" button. The interviewee eyed the machine dubiously, but then took on an expression of readiness to face the worst.

Sid felt a little ridiculous as she opened her notebook. Imagine yourself in a play, she told herself. You're just doing a role, the part of an eager young anthroplogist. No sweat.

"Mr. Prow, like I said on the phone, I've been here less than two years, and it seemed as if you'd be a good person to go to for information on the theater—the building itself and . . . things."

He smiled and nodded, munching a Twinkie. "There's not much about that place I don't know, that's certain."

"How long have you been there?"

"Oh, I'd say it'd be about fifteen years now. I started about the time my son, Clem, joined me in the garage business. Had a little free time then and figured I could use it earning more money."

"And you've been doing all the cleaning and fixing since then?"

"Yep. It helps to have someone about who really knows a place, 'specially an old place like that. They built 'em sound in them days, but they did have some funny ways of putting things together. You got to know it. Like when they had this electrician fellow and I was the only one could show him where them old wires run."

"That's very interesting. Mr. Prow . . ."

"George. You call me George in the theater when you're running around in war paint, so you can call me George in my home."

Sid smiled awkwardly. "Okay, George. You said the theater was an old one. Do you know how old?"

"1883. That's what the plaque said before somebody stole it."

"That's pretty old. I know there's a tradition in a lot of theaters about their being haunted. It's supposed to be sort of good luck. In the fifteen years you've worked there, have you . . . well, have you ever seen anything like that?"

"Have I ever seen a ghost there?" He laughed like dry crackling leaves. "You ain't gonna turn this stuff over to a bunch of doctors that'd haul an old man away, are you?"

"No, no! This is only an English class paper."

"Well, sure, I'll tell you. Ain't no secret, I suppose. I seen ghosts in that place, plenty of times. Kind of put the wind up me at first, I tell you. But they don't cause nobody no harm. I just sort of ignore 'em now."

Sid was excited and a little alarmed. She'd half expected, half hoped maybe, that this would be a dead end. Nervously she took a big swallow of Coke.

"What are they like?"

"Well, that's kind of hard to say. Just little bunches of mist mostly. Sometimes they look like people though, kind of gray and washed out, like old photographs maybe. And sometimes I don't see 'em as much as I feel 'em. Kind of cold like. You know something's there, even if you don't feel nothing."

Sid shivered, remembering the spiral stairs. "Did you see them when you first started working there?"

He frowned thoughtfully. "No, can't say as I did. Maybe it took 'em a while to get used to me or something. Guess I only started noticing 'em about eight or ten years ago."

"You don't sound like they scare you very much."

"Well, no, not anymore. I mean a person don't like having them sorts of things hanging around. But they don't do no harm. Don't even seem to notice me. They just git about their business, whatever that is, and I git about mine."

"That's awfully brave of you. Do you know if other people in the theater have seen them?"

"Well, I expect they has, but probably just thought they was imagining things. But mostly they don't show up unless the place's pretty quiet and empty, and usually I'm the only person around then."

He took a big swig of coffee, then laughed. "Now if you're really wanting a good grade on this paper of yours, all you got to do is spend a night alone in that theater. Take that machine of yours. Not that they make much noise. One does though. Can't say I like him none. But they won't harm you, and you'll sure have something to write about."

Alarmed at the suggestion, Sid gulped down some more Coke. Then she cleared her throat. "Well I guess I could do that. But I've already got a lot of information here. You've been very helpful."

"Well, I'm happy to be. Got a granddaughter who's always asking grandpa about the 'old days.' I tells her some true stuff and some tall tales, too. So mind you don't go around telling folks at the theater that old George sees ghosts. If you do, now, I'll tell 'em I was pulling your leg."

31

"No, no, don't worry. I'll just put it in my paper, and only my teacher will see it."

After politely eating a stale Twinkie and thanking her informant again, Sid gathered up her equipment. She gave Daisy a tentative pat on the head and took her leave.

Outside, a few splatters of rain blew from the lead gray sky. The wind was snatching off tattered maple leaves and hurling them through the air. Sid pulled up the collar of her jacket and headed home, fighting to tuck in the strands of dark hair that fluttered about her face.

She was excited, but she wasn't sure whether it was happy excitement or not. She'd gotten some good material for her paper. But now there couldn't be any doubt that the theater *was* haunted. Of course she'd seen something and so had Joel, but having a grown-up confirm it, sort of made it final. The problem was, she wasn't sure if she really *liked* having a haunted theater, good luck or not.

And she certainly wished George hadn't talked about spending a night at the theater. That was the sort of dumb thing kids did in books. "I dare you to spend a night in the old graveyard." Stupid! But try as she might, she couldn't quite shake the idea from her head.

The sky had darkened with clouds and coming night. Trees loomed like dark skeletons against the sky, and the wind moaned through their leafless branches. She hurried on. This was definitely not the setting for thinking about that sort of thing.

CHAPTER

The next day the sun was out again, but it was a pale wintery sun. It shown weakly on bare branches and on puddle-splotched roads. The wind was cold. Sid hurried home. She hadn't dragged her winter jacket from the back closet yet, but the time had clearly come.

In English today, they'd had to turn in the topics of their papers along with a brief outline and sources. She'd tried to keep hers pretty vague. The teacher had hardly glanced at the outlines, but had said that they should use both oral and written sources. Lots of luck! Where was she going to find something written about their haunted theater?

Once inside her yard, she knelt to give Fred his regular greeting. Glancing up through the shop window, she saw that her mother had a man with her. Not Byron Vincenti again! She didn't know why she felt so uneasy about that man. Everyone else thought he was gorgeous, and Becky practically swooned at his name. Yet she still felt he was missing something, like a half-finished portrait.

Once in the front hall, she peeped cautiously through the door and was relieved and surprised to see it was Rev. Aikens sitting with her mother at a book-strewn table. The two looked up, and the minister smiled from under his big mustache.

"Hello, Sidonie. I've finally gotten around to cleaning out the parsonage library. Some real treasures, but theologically not quite up-to-date. These I thought, would be better off here where collectors might buy them from your mother."

Sid dropped her bookbag onto a leather hassock. "That's nice of you, Rev. Aikens. Any old romantic novels with soppy pictures?"

Mrs. Guthrie laughed. "It doesn't look as if Rev. Aikens's predecessors read that sort of thing."

"Or if they did, they didn't keep the evidence," he added as he pulled out another large leather-bound book from the box at his feet. "This is more their style, *A Minister's Handbook For All Manner of Dealings With Ghosts, Witches, and Other Phenomena of the Supernatural*. It looks as if we once had a preacher here something like those crazy ministers in that play of yours."

Sid was interested now. "Does it really tell how to deal with ghosts?"

He chuckled. "It's strictly for professionals. No mass-market exorcisms. Everything a minister needs to know about ghosts and ghoulies. Really incredible."

Mrs. Guthrie opened the book and carefully flipped through the pages. "It's not very worn. Doesn't look like our local ministers had much call for this sort of thing."

"Well, I certainly haven't been called upon for any exorcisms yet," he said, laughing. "If I am, maybe I can borrow it back. All I know is how they do it in the movies."

He pulled out another book then stopped. "Though, come to think of it, there could have been some use for that. I was reading Rev. Farley's journal a while ago—he was minister here around the turn of the century—and he mentioned there were supposed to be ghosts in that theater of yours. And then he said—you'll love this—he said he refused to meddle in the matter. If citizens chose to involve themselves in such immoral activities as the stage, they deserved whatever spiritual confrontations they got."

Mrs. Guthrie looked at her daughter. "Sid, isn't that . . ."

"Yes it is! And that's terrific because our teacher says we need written sources! You see, Rev. Aikens, I'm doing this Hoosier folklore paper about our haunted theater. Where did you find that? Can I use it as a source?"

"Certainly. I'm glad the old fellow's journal is of some use. I have to keep that one as part of church records, but you can say it's from the journal of Rev. Charles W. Farley." Sid scurried for a paper and pencil as he continued. "He was minister here from 1895 to 1911, I think. The entry where he mentioned the theater was maybe 1907 or '08. Probably 1907 since he went on to talk about inspecting the new parsonage, and that was built in '07."

Sid beamed. "Thanks a lots. That's exactly what I need."

The minister pulled a final three books out of his box. "Someone ought to be interested in these. One's a 1902 geography of Africa. Probably for finding their missionaries. Here's a book on birds of the Bible lands; nice pictures. Then there's a 1921 practical guide for building outhouses. Wonderful!"

He stood up, and Sid's mother did the same. "I just can't thank you enough," she said. "Are you sure I can't pay you something for them?"

"No. I needed the shelf space, and you mightn't be able to get rid of them. Not exactly best sellers."

"Oh, I'm sure we'll find them good homes. Thank you again, Rev. Aikens."

"I may have another batch for you after spring cleaning. And it doesn't have to be 'Reverend Aikens.' Dennis will do."

"All right, Dennis."

Sid sort of liked the way her mother smiled at him as she said that.

Sid hummed as she washed the lettuce, thinking fondly of last night's tryouts for *Ruddigore*. She'd felt like an old-timer among the scattering of awestruck newcomers. Not that anybody with half a voice was ever turned down for chorus. This was "community theater" after all, and if their chorus of mixed ages and shapes didn't look like a matched Broadway group, at least the community was having fun in theater.

It had been even more fun watching the tryouts for lead parts. Mrs. Nolton had been livid when the part of Rose Maybud had gone to Sid's mother and not her own daughter, Viola.

Sid smiled. She had to hand it to that director. Not many people could stand up to Mrs. Nolton. And now her mother was going to sing soprano lead. The only problem was that Byron Vincenti had been cast as the male lead. Still, he seemed to have come out of the moody funk he'd been in since *The Crucible*. And this was a much happier play, even if his new character was rather erratically demented.

She began tearing the lettuce into a salad bowl. Last night she'd kept her eyes open but hadn't seen any wispy nothings lurking in corners. Maybe George was right; they kept out of the way when things were active and noisy.

The thought of George sent a frown across her face. She wished he'd never mentioned staying overnight in the theater. Her paper was due soon; and now that the place felt friendly again, it was hard to justify not trying it. Besides, she had to admit, it might be fun.

Her mother, draining the spaghetti, had picked up the tune Sid was humming, and with an exchange of smiles, the two burst into the *Ruddigore* chorus of ancestral ghosts.

*"When the night wind howls, in the chimney cowls, and
    the bat in the moonlight flies,
And inky clouds, like funeral shrouds, sail over the
    midnight skies,
When the footpads quail at the nightbirds' wail, and
    the black dog bays at the moon,
Then is the spectres holiday, then is the ghosts' high
    noon."*

On the "oo" of "noon", Sid slid dramatically down the
scale like howling wind. Her mother laughed, plunking the
tureen of spaghetti on the white kitchen table.

"A pity all the really fun Gilbert and Sullivan songs go to
the men. You do that beautifully."

Sid took her seat and reached for the shaker of Parmesan
cheese. "Speaking of ghosts, Mom, you remember my
paper on the haunted theater?"

"Yes. And I guess with six local guys playing the
Ruddigore ghosts, it can't help but be haunted now."

Sid forced a laugh. "Yeah, but this is supposed to be *real*
ghosts. I've done interviews, and thanks to Rev. Aikens
I've got a written source. But I need one more thing."

"Oh?"

"Field research."

Her mother looked noncommittal and continued eating
her tossed salad. "How do you propose to do that?"

"Well, this Wednesday, there's no school because of
teacher training. So I thought that Tuesday night I could
take my sleeping bag, notebook, and tape recorder over to
the theater and spend the night."

"But . . ."

"It'll be perfectly safe. The theater's locked up at night.
Then I could wait and see if any ghosts appear, and record
everything on the spot. It's all I need to really *make* my term
paper."

"Well . . . I don't think the board . . ."

37

"They don't have to know about it. I'm keeping most of my sources officially anonymous."

Her mother chewed a bite of French bread. "Actually, I do have a key. I forgot to return it after working on those costumes last spring."

"Great! Then I can run a real scientific experiment and turn out a first-class paper."

Sid was feeling slightly less confident on Tuesday night when, with sleeping bag and pack, she hiked over to the theater. There were no chorus rehearsals there that night, and the principals were working at the house of Ginny Albers, who had the part of Mad Margaret as well as the best piano in town.

The night was cold and blustery. Overhead, a pale half moon seemed to fly behind ragged wind-driven clouds. The wind rattled through skeletal branches and moaned through utility wires.

The brooding bulk of the theater loomed up in the darkness, striking Sid with a wave of doubt. In the flickering moon shadows, the limestone cupids above the door leered demonically.

Sid took a deep breath and stuck the key into the door. She almost hoped it wouldn't work, but melodramatically the door creaked open. She stepped into the waiting darkness, cringing against the expected touch of icy fingers.

Nothing happened. She was greeted instead with the familiar smell of the theater. What made it, she didn't know; but it was a special smell, unique to this place, and it always filled her with a thrill of excitement. This is where it happened, where fantasy became reality. Here special people came together to create something special, something that other people enjoyed. This was her theater.

Confident again, she flipped on a hall light and made her way backstage. After eyeing the spiral stairs, she convinced herself that because of her pack and bag, the roomy back stairs were more practical.

She had decided to make her research camp in the costume loft. With colorful clothing hung all around, it was warm and cozy. And she had to admit, it felt safer.

Once she'd trudged up the backstairs, she switched on the light and surveyed her choice of a campsite, a compromise between security and research. She grabbed hold of a rather deflated floor pillow used for a harem atmosphere in *Kismet*, and crammed it between a wall, a large box of fabric scraps, and the mesh fence that formed the side of the loft overlooking the stage.

After unrolling her sleeping bag, she pulled a flashlight from her pack and walked back to switch off the loft light. Returning to her nest she began her vigil, punctuated by an occasional dip into a bag of chocolate cookies.

In the darkness, time dragged by. She tried to fill it by recalling lines from *The Crucible* but soon stopped: the subject definitely created the wrong mood.

She concentrated instead on listening. She was a rabbit snug in its burrow, listening for every possible threatening sound. Up here close to the roof, the main sound was the wind blowing in fitful gusts, rattling loose metal shingles like tuneless windchimes.

But if she tried to filter that out, she could hear other sounds. The occasional creakings and saggings of an old building. No dragging chains, though, and no mournful moanings. With the wind and the creaking it was like riding in an old sailing ship, rocking snug and secure in the cabin.

She jerked her head up. This was no good, she was falling asleep. She beamed her flashlight down onto the stage. Nothing. But she couldn't see quite all of the stage from here. Besides, maybe these things didn't stay just around the stage. Hadn't her mother felt something in a dressing room?

Resolutely she gripped her flashlight, slung her tape recorder onto a shoulder and stood up, stretching her cramped legs. She'd go on a tour of inspection.

By the flashlight beam, she picked her way down to the catwalk, then deliberately headed for the spiral stairs. Cautiously she stepped onto the top step but heard or felt nothing on the stairs below. Then quickly before she lost her nerve, she started down, her winding descent setting off a round of metallic groaning.

At the bottom she began walking across the stage, crisscrossing it in a scientific grid. She shone her light everywhere but saw nothing ominous. Just empty stage, curtains, ropes, and a few pieces of set leaning against the dark painted walls.

She stopped at last in the center of the stage and felt the same bubbling thrill that always came at this spot. She closed her eyes and tried to imagine the dark hall bursting with light and life. The empty seats were filled with people, people enjoying the play, enjoying her performance. With the stage flooded with light, she stood in the center wearing a shapely spangled costume, graciously taking the applause. She bowed, and the applause rose. It rose to the rafters then sank, sank to a whisper.

She opened her eyes. The theater was empty, dark, and silent. Silent except for the whispers. She spun around. On the floor against the back wall, grayness seemed to blow like snow, blow with the dry whispering of drifting snow.

She stepped forward. The grayness thinned and sighed and slowly wasn't there. She stood frozen, torn between searching and fleeing. The former was losing.

Abruptly she turned around, then almost screamed. A young man stood on the stage. His clothes were black, and his blond hair fell to his shoulders. He walked silently across the stage not seeing her. Then slowly his gaunt anguished face turned her way. The eyes were large and dark. They opened into a great dark emptiness. Pulled by that darkness, Sid felt a cold grip tightening around her, drawing her into endless nothing.

The emptiness shattered into a scream. Her scream. Deaf to the noise, the specter walked on, dissolving into the black folds of a curtain.

Sid's heart hammered in her chest and her whole body was damp with sweat. She wanted to run, but the only movement she seemed capable of was shivering.

Closing her eyes, she took several deep breaths. Slowly, her body calmed. She took a few slow steps to prove that she could. Perhaps it was time to leave now. Just walk out the door and head home. She'd think about how silly and cowardly that was later.

As though to taunt her, the theater still echoed with her scream. But that couldn't be. She listened and heard the wind shrieking outside the walls. Still there was something more. A sound almost beyond hearing. And it came from way in the back of the theater.

She brought up her flashlight and shone it back and forth across the empty seats. Suddenly it stopped. A sound and shape were forming at the back of the left aisle.

It was the shape of a man, a man in golden robes, and over his head he held something. A sword. A keening wail, high and scarcely audible, seemed to rise from the apparition. It moved forward slowly, like something in a slow-motion film. Steadily, he and the scream came closer.

Suddenly remembering the tape recorder, Sid switched it on. That mundane action seemed to break her trance. As the wailing, sword-brandishing specter moved closer to the stage, she backed up. It reached the orchestra pit and in an astonishing slow motion leap it vaulted over, glowing robes floating about it like billowing seaweed.

It landed on the stage and kept moving, moving toward her. She turned and ran back to the spiral stairs, her screams

41

blending with its wail. She felt as if she were running in glue, running in a dream. She had to get away from it and couldn't move fast enough.

She crawled up the stairs, pulling herself up every turn. It was behind her now, coming closer. Another turn and another.

She dragged herself up onto the metal catwalk, just as the shrieking glowing thing rushed past her, along the catwalk and then out into empty space. It glided thirty feet above the stage, then vanished through the far wall.

Sid found herself walking; the walk turned into a run until she was up in the loft and diving into her sleeping bag. She pulled the top over her and jerked the drawstring closed.

In the snug darkness, she hugged herself, trying not to think. But thought came. Was this the noise-making ghost old George had hinted at? Was this a fuller form of what she had felt before on those stairs?

She wanted to be home now, but couldn't make herself walk through that theater again, not for anything. She stuck out a hand, rustled in the cookie bag, then sucking on a chocolate cookie, she fell asleep.

CHAPTER

Sid woke suddenly to the sound of a voice. And she knew it was a human voice, although it rang through the theater like a trumpet.

Cautiously she poked her head out of her cocoon. She recognized that voice. It was Byron Vincenti.

Shifting her body quietly, she peered through the fencing to the stage below. The work lights had been switched on, and Byron stood in the middle of the stage reciting lines. Sid recognized them: Ruthven Murgatroyd's lines from *Ruddigore*.

Relief washed over her. Byron couldn't sleep, so he'd come here to rehearse his lines in the usual setting. Eccentric, perhaps, but reassuringly human.

Then her elation faded. There seemed to be others down there too, others that were less than human. The shapes of some were gray and cloudy. Others had sharper outlines. She recognized a few. The young man in black was there, drifting in and out of the light, those empty eyes always fixed on Byron. The screamer was silent now but seemed to float and swoop over the actor's head.

Sid squinted, trying to bring the blurry shapes into focus. There was a black man in opulent robes and a turban. There was a figure in sailor white and another in Puritan black.

Had she seen that one before? Others were too vague to focus on.

She watched and realized with astonishment that these specters were not behaving as before. Earlier, though she had been terrified by their presence, they had ignored her. Old George had said they just went about their business, and Joel had noted that they even seemed oblivious of each other. But now they were clustered around Byron like moths around a light. They seemed to watch his every move.

For his part, Byron clearly knew they were there. Occasionally he swiped at them when they came too close, or swatted at the swooping one as if it were an annoying insect. That was it! He seemed more annoyed than frightened, as though they were bothersome but familiar.

Entranced, Sid watched while minute after minute passed. Byron was getting into the scene where Ruthven Murgatroyd confronts his ghostly ancestors. It was a somewhat comic scene, but in the present setting it seemed anything but comic.

Suddenly the actor whirled around and shook his fist at the clustering forms. He bellowed the next line in a fury, totally out of keeping with the scene.

"Oh stop! Stop it, will you? I can't stand it!"

He turned and stomped off the stage. The figures shimmered and faded away, even before the lights were switched off. An outside door opened and closed.

Still hesitant to leave her refuge, Sid stayed awake the rest of the night finishing the cookies and moving on to a bag of potato chips. Outside the wind howled fitfully, but inside the theater she saw and heard nothing more unusual than a single scurrying mouse.

The hands of her watch finally crept toward six A.M. From beyond the walls she could hear a few hearty winter birds taking up the dawn chorus. Gratefully, she packed up, and hurried down the backstairs and along the corridor to the front lobby.

She was almost at the door when a memory jumped at her. She stopped and flashed her light over the lobby walls, where photos of plays from previous seasons hung. There was the one she sought! One she had seen regularly but never really paid any attention to—until now.

It was from *Hamlet*, produced several seasons before she and her mother had come here. To stage right by a carved oaken chair, stood a young man in black. Blond hair hung to his shoulders, and his face was gaunt and familiar. Only the eyes were different from those she had seen. They were human eyes. Almost reluctantly she dropped her gaze to the typed caption. "Hamlet, played by Byron Vincenti."

That Saturday, Sid and her mother went to the theater at noon. Everyone in the cast was considered part of the set crew. But for Sid, set work was more than a duty. She loved seeing how all the parts of a show went together. It was as much fun as acting—almost.

When they arrived, wooden frames had been nailed together for scenery flats, and some were already covered with canvas. Several artistic sorts, with charcoal stick in one hand and a rendering of the set in the other, were sketching rough outlines onto the flats. Mrs. Guthrie soon joined those mixing paint, and Sid wandered off to find Joel.

She located him in the carpentry shop, hammering together an extra-large picture frame. The air was filled with the warm woody smell of sawdust. Hammers thumped, saws screeched, and voices yelled over the din. As Joel stepped back to appraise his work, Sid handed him a manila envelope.

"A copy of my paper. I thought you might like to read it."

He flashed her a conspiratorial grin. "I trust you have been discreet."

"Don't worry. I gave everyone aliases like in police stories."

He peered into the envelope. "Good. If word ever got around school that I'd been seeing . . . well, what I've been seeing, I'd never hear the end of it."

Sid returned to where the flats were spread over the stage floor. For a while she helped Stan, the shoe-store clerk, paint roses on a garden wall. Then she moved on to one of the ancestor portraits. She'd just finished the curled-up mustache when Joel came up behind her.

"Nice job, even if that collar does make it look like Bill's head is on a platter."

She swung around, flicking paint on his already mangled shoes. "At least it's more artistic than hammering boards together."

"Ah, but these frames are ingenious. Do you know how they work?"

"No. I just do what I'm told and ask no questions."

"Where is your spirit of inquiry? There'll be a rod down each picture that fits into the frame. During the first part of the scene, the actor stands behind the picture of himself. Then when I kill the lights, he pivots the thing around to the blank side and stands in front in the same pose."

"Ingenious."

"I read your paper."

"Ingenious?"

"Not bad. I noticed a few things left out, though."

"Right." She lowered her voice. "Well, the tape recording wasn't worth much. You could hardly tell what was my scream and what was the other. And I couldn't very well mention what I saw happening that night with Byron. I mean, the paper is hard enough to believe with all those 'anonymous sources.' That other just sounds crazy."

Joel glanced about him, then answered quietly. "I sure don't understand that bit. Byron could be tied up with these . . . these things somehow. But all we can do, I guess, in good detective fashion, is 'keep our eyes open.'"

Sid intended to do that. However, mysteries in real life weren't proving as manageable as those in books. There, one event usually ran logically into another. But here, she didn't have the faintest idea what should happen next.

During dinner she fretted over the problem. It was only toward the end of the meal that she noticed her mother seemed equally distracted. As she served up the Jell-O, Mrs. Guthrie said with forced casualness, "I guess I'm going on sort of a date tonight, Sidonie."

Startled, Sid looked up, then immediately dropped her eyes and sliced her spoon into her wobbly red dessert. "Oh?"

"Yes, Byron asked me out for coffee and to talk about the play, though, Lord knows, we get enough of that at rehearsals."

She smiled tensely, and Sid returned a quick uncertain smile. It was fine for her mother to be dating, she told herself. She was pretty and the sort who obviously needs people. But Byron Vincenti? Admittedly, half the females in town would gladly trade places with her mother. And Becky would be beside herself tomorrow if she heard about it. But none of them knew certain things about the man. Of course, Sid realized, she really didn't *know* them either.

"Okay," Sid said, swallowing a spoonful of Jell-O. "If you want to go up and get ready, I'll do the dishes."

Her mother looked relieved and took her up on the offer. By the time Sid had finished drying, Mrs. Guthrie was downstairs again wearing a blue silk dress Sid hadn't seen on her for two years. When the doorbell rang, Sid called good-bye from the kitchen. What was she supposed to do, stand at the door and tell her mother not to stay out late?

47

Sid felt restless in the empty house. For once her math homework didn't take long enough. She switched on the TV and watched part of an old movie about seances and Ouija boards. After a while she turned it off and went up to bed. She didn't need to see spooky stuff on TV, too.

She got ready for bed slowly, wanting irrationally to stay up until her mother got back. But at last she put the lights out and lay in bed listening to the wind blow about the house. Like a curious beast, it rattled the windows and doors as though looking for a way in. It was almost as if something were out there, Sid thought, something trying to get in—at her. She pulled the comforter over her head, and in the warm darkness scolded herself for being too old for this sort of thing.

Around midnight she woke to the sound of the front door closing, or rather slamming, and her mother's quick, angry-sounding footsteps coming up the stairs. After a while she thought she heard the muffled sound of crying from her mother's room.

The next morning at breakfast, Sid didn't know whether to say something or not. Finally she decided on the "supportive approach."

"The date didn't go too well last night?"

Her mother looked surprised for a moment, then clumped her coffee mug down on the table. A little hot brown liquid slopped onto her toast.

"No, not really. I shouldn't let him affect me so, but I just don't understand Byron. Sometimes he's so nice and almost fragile-seeming, and other times . . . I just never know what to expect of him. But he can certainly be a haughty, egotistical jerk when he wants to be! Honestly, he's just like that character he's playing. One moment he's absolutely despicable, and the next he's so charming he practically sweeps you off your feet."

Suddenly she laughed, looking at her daughter. "Now

48

there's role-reversal for you! The mother griping about her date to the teenage daughter. I'm sorry, Sid, I shouldn't unload on you."

"Don't be," Sid said, standing up to hide her own embarrassment. "People with gripes should gripe."

Mrs. Guthrie stood up and hugged her daughter. "Sage advice, worthy of a newspaper column. But I can almost hear some old biddies now: 'What is the American family coming to?' "

Sid smiled. "Oh, ours is coming along all right." She completed the thought to herself—as long as nobody creepy interferes.

CHAPTER

As soon as Sid slammed off the alarm Monday morning, she felt that something was different. Lying in bed she tried to focus her drowsy thoughts on what it was. It seemed lighter than it should be when the alarm went off. Quickly, she squinted at her clock. No, she had not overslept. She stretched luxuriously under the covers and lay quiet again.

Then suddenly she knew. The silence. Deep silence, as though all the world's little background sounds had been turned off. That plus the light could only mean one thing.

Jumping out of bed she padded barefoot across the cold floorboards to the window and thrust aside the curtain. Snow! It had snowed during the night, the year's first real snowfall. And it was still falling, falling in big white flakes.

Bursting with the news, she ran across the landing to her mother's bedroom, and found her just fumbling with her own pealing alarm clock.

"It snowed! Lots!"

Her mother smiled vaguely and showed little enthusiasm for getting out of bed. But soon both, clad in their nightgowns, were standing by the window.

"It's cold and it's a bother," her mother observed, "but it certainly is lovely."

"A bother? Snow is wonderful!"

"Think of the slush. Think of all the time it takes to get dressed. Think . . ."

"No don't. Think how beautiful it makes everything. Besides, snow here stays pretty. It doesn't get all sooty and gray like in cities. And they might have to close school!"

At the thought, Sid rushed for her bathrobe and scurried downstairs to turn on the kitchen radio. Music, then an ad for used cars, then the school reports. All local schools would be open, except in the county to the east.

"That's not fair!" Sid protested. "We never close for snow!"

"That's because our school board members are a bunch of macho jerks," her mother observed matter-of-factly as she opened the refrigerator.

"Well, if things stay open, at least rehearsal won't be canceled," Sid said, grasping at the small consolation.

By seven o'clock that evening the snow had stopped and the scene was reduced to Christmas-card stillness. This was a chorus rehearsal, so after dinner, only Sid struggled into her jacket, boots, hat, mittens, and scarf. And as always happened when Sid went to the theater alone, her mother insisted on her taking Fred. Sid regularly protested that no one was ever mugged around here. But Mrs. Guthrie's city ways were ingrained, and Fred went along.

The snow seemed to freeze away the dog's usual lethargy, and, as far as the leash allowed, he frolicked in the little white drifts. But he still didn't look ferocious. Sid couldn't imagine what good he would be if someone actually did try to mug her.

The rehearsal went well enough, although several members were out with colds. When the women's chorus was dismissed, Sid went to the lobby to retrieve Fred and found him as she had left him, chin resting on two crossed paws.

As they stepped out of the theater's main entrance, Sid almost gasped at the scene before her. The sky had been swept clean of clouds, and into it had risen a full moon. The silver moonlight mirrored by the snow, lit everything nearly like day, except that there was a different quality to the light, a cold unreality. It created a realm of magic things, things that had nothing to do with daylight.

As Sid stood enraptured, Evelyn Bidwell bustled past her. "You need a ride, Sidonie?"

She blinked, "Oh, no. No thank you, Mrs. Bidwell. I have Fred here for escort, and it's an absolutely beautiful night for a walk."

"Umm, yes it is isn't it? Well, take care, dear. See you Wednesday."

Sid stood on the steps until the various cars had roared off. Behind her, she could hear the faint rumbling of the men's chorus, but the world outside was completely still. The glittering white snow seemed to have muffled any sound, and even the air was frozen into stillness.

"Come on, Fred," she whispered. "Let's take the long way home."

They set off through the snow. Though not deep, it made light sparkling plumes as they kicked it. Fred lunged at these and at his own cavorting shadow.

As they rounded the corner of the building, they saw a man coming out of the theater's side door. Sid could tell from his striding walk and his outlandishly theatrical cape, that it was Byron Vincenti. He'd come in tonight to work with the chorus.

Sid tensed and slowed her pace as the actor walked east around the back of the building. When he reached the alley, she expected him to head north in the direction of his modest little home on the town's outskirts. But instead he turned south, the direction Sid had planned to go.

She stopped for a moment, then angrily forged ahead. She wasn't going to let creepy Mr. Vincenti ruin her moonlight walk.

52

When she and Fred reached the east end of the building, she could see Byron passing Mrs. Clement's snow-mantled garden. But by the time they reached that spot, the dark figure ahead of them had vanished.

As they walked on, Sid marveled at how the moonlight and snow changed everything. Familiar, ordinary things like sheds, fences, and even garbage cans looked strange and beautiful. The shadows the moon cast on the snow were as sharp and black as obsidian.

They were just passing between the church and the little cemetery when Sid stopped short. Fred looked back at her inquiringly, but she took no notice.

Her eyes were on the shapes and shadows beyond the graveyard walls. Where everything else in the world was still, there something moved. Between the tombstones and the stark leafless trees, a shadow passed. Byron Vincenti had gone into the graveyard.

Sid stood rooted in the snow like a frozen tree. All her pleasure in the night shriveled into dread. She recalled the scene of the empty stage with Byron Vincenti standing amid swirling ghostly shapes. What was he doing now in a graveyard?

She tried to shake off a cold cloak of fear. This was just like some Nancy Drew mystery, she told herself. Young girl detective follows sinister figure into graveyard to see what he is up to. Almost automatically Sid moved toward the cemetery. However, she reminded herself, Nancy Drew always got into a pack of trouble, and she, Sid Guthrie, had no convenient author to get her out again. She certainly had no intention of actually following someone *into* a grave-yard. Not at night, and not this someone.

The shadowy figure ahead had stopped near the center of the cemetery between a large marble angel and a tombstone carved like a dead tree. Sid stopped outside the wall, which, edged in deep shadow, now seemed a substantial and welcome barrier. Snow frosted its jagged top and filled the chinks between stones. She crouched behind it and a clawlike dogwood, which, in the frozen winter night, seemed as dead as the tombstones.

From behind these dubious defenses, she could see Byron seated upon an arched headstone. He was saying something over and over again, like a chant.

The hair along her arms prickled. Was this some sort of incantation? Was he calling up the dead? Fearfully she glanced down at Fred, expecting to see him wide-eyed and cringing with fear. But having determined his mistress wasn't going on, Fred had plunked himself into the snow and closed his eyes for a nap. Well, she thought angrily, either this stuff about dogs being uncannily sensitive to the supernatural was a lot of baloney, or Fred was a dud, the exception to the rule.

Clutching at the rough bark of the tree trunk, Sid strained to hear what Byron was saying. She could only catch a word here and there. Suddenly his voice rose dramatically. He was reciting lines from *Ruddigore!*

Had he come all this way out here for a quiet place to rehearse? What a fanatic! She almost laughed, when suddenly he swirled his cape aside and pulled out the prop bullwhip. He launched into the song from the Act I finale, the one punctuated by cracks of the whip.

Sid, hidden in the spidery tree shadow, stared at the bizarre scene before her. It was a surrealistic play set; all stark whites and inky blacks, bathed in eerie moonglow. Amid shadow-edged crosses and statues, the Bad Baronet of Ruddigore stood singing and shouting and cracking a whip.

The scene was mad, an insane dream. And suddenly Sid realized that it was not the scene perhaps, but the man that was mad. And what was she doing out here, alone, watching him?

The night's shattered silence now stirred with a new sound. Behind her, a wind had risen. She could hear it whooshing up the hill from the west. It was time to go.

She tugged on Fred's leash, but he was already sitting up, pressed close against her leg, shivering. Wide-eyed, he stared not into the graveyard, but behind her.

Sid spun around. On the wind, from the direction of the theater, came a roiling mist—a tattered patch of gray, its tendrils coiling into shapes that were almost human. It drew closer, and Sid sank down against the wall and the whimpering dog.

The things passed unnoticing overhead. She saw them, gray and horrid through the bare branches, before they swirled off to the center of the cemetery. Byron threw up his arms and filled the night with a string of curses. Then he flung down the whip and shouted, "Fie, foul spirits! Why do you torment me? Fly, go hence!"

Sounded like Shakespeare, maybe. Sid didn't know. But she did know that *she* was going hence.

Crouching low, she tugged at Fred's leash. In seconds they were pelting over the ground as fast as the cloying snow allowed. They reached the sheltering shadow of the church but kept running on to the street. Normally, Fred would have objected to the pace, but now Sid had to hold him back. They trotted jerkily along, their breath rising in quick white puffs.

There was no doubt about it, Sid thought, the man her mother was getting involved with was himself involved in something very, very wrong. He was either a witch or a madman. And in either case, something, somehow, had to be done.

Thursday afternoon, Sid persuaded her mother to drive her the twelve miles to the county seat. She had to do research for a paper, she said, and the school library just wasn't adequate. Sid visited the county library pretty regularly and doubted that her mother would guess this particular paper was fictitious.

Mrs. Guthrie dropped Sid off in front of the old brick building, saying she'd be back in an hour and a half. Shabby and overcrowded, the structure still showed some of its turn-of-the-century grandeur. With the eagerness of a hound following a scent, Sid hurried up the worn stone steps.

She went directly to the massive oak card catalogue in the main lobby. Pulling out a "W" drawer, she flipped quickly through Water and Will, to Witch. Taking a notebook from her bag, she began copying the call numbers of everything having to do with witchcraft, not the fiction or the collections of spooky stories, but the more serious stuff.

Judging by their call numbers, she realized they'd all be grouped. After some searching, she found the right shelf on the third-floor stacks. But there was nothing. All the books had been checked out except one on the Salem witch trials, and she already knew all she wanted about that.

Discouraged, Sid walked back to the main desk. The librarian looked up.

"May I help you?"

"Maybe. I'm doing a report on witchcraft, and all the books I need are checked out. If I give you the numbers, could you tell me who they're out to? If any are out to someone I know, maybe I can borrow them."

The librarian shook her head. "Normally we don't do that. But you're a regular here. I guess I can see if some are out to anyone you're likely to know."

She took Sid's list and turned to a file drawer. After a minute checking through cards, she said, "One book, *Witches, Witches, and More Witches*, is checked out to a girl here in town. But the rest are out to someone who lives near you. Do you know a Byron Vincenti?"

Sid felt as if she'd swallowed a gallon of ice water. "Oh. Yes. I know Byron. Thanks."

For a moment she stood frowning by the desk. On impulse, she went back to the card catalogue and repeated the process with "Ghosts." Only two of those books were *not* on the shelves.

But if Byron Vincenti had no interest in these, then neither did she. She hadn't expected to find this, but it did bolster an idea that had been nagging at her. Maybe this wasn't an "ordinary haunting." Maybe, somehow, Byron Vincenti had conjured up these spirits. What they were dealing with here was not ghosts, but witchcraft.

Dress week arrived, the last week before the show opened. They had rehearsals every night. But it seemed impossible that everything would be ready by Friday night. For the first time, the cast was rehearsing with the orchestra. The violins squeaked painfully, and the pace was funereal. When the choruses slowed for the musicians, the whole thing sounded like a record on the wrong speed. The director was tearing out his hair.

He had also had a last-minute inspiration that in the finale the bridesmaids should weave garlands around the loving couples in an intertwining May dance. This meant that a vast number of crepe paper flowers had to be made and sewn onto ribbons. It also meant that the final scene had to be reblocked. Sid feared she'd never learn to dip over and under at the right points. The effect so far was of kittens going for a ball of yarn.

Friday crept closer. Some costumes still didn't fit. Sid was glad hers wouldn't be seen up close. The lace was loose on her cuffs, and the hem, which she'd had to raise herself, was woefully uneven. She thought Viola Nolton's costume was far too tight. But Viola seemed to like the visual effect of being squeezed out the top like toothpaste. Sid guessed she'd never give that effect herself, no matter how tight her bodice.

Finally opening night arrived. An hour before the show, everyone was flitting nervously around backstage, getting into costumes, makeup, and each other's way. The stage crew was daubing paint on unfinished scenery, while the stage manager frantically warned the cast which bits not to touch.

Then it was five minutes to curtain time. Everyone took their places in the wings and listened to the orchestra squeak and boom through the overture. Actually, they were getting better, Sid thought, trying to suppress her own stage fright by being the detached critic. It didn't work. Her palms were so sweaty, she was afraid to touch her costume.

Then the orchestra finished with a flourish, the curtains were hauled open, and from both wings the bridesmaids tripped in, giggling demurely, and at a note from the orchestra, broke into song. Thereafter, Sid was swept up in the ridiculous musical dilemmas of maids and ghosts and star-crossed lovers, and before she'd even realized that this was *it,* the real thing, the performance was over.

It was only when she'd finally gotten into bed and was beginning to unwind, that she realized she hadn't given a thought to the real supernatural events in the place. She hadn't looked for whispering shadows crouching in corners and had paid attention to Byron Vincenti only as dashing Ruthven Murgatroyd, not as a crazed actor who conjures spirits on the side.

That, she decided sleepily, was the way she'd like to keep it.

That determination, however, like opening night euphoria, did not last. She couldn't help noticing that after every show Byron hung around even past the resetting of the stage, saying he wanted to stay a while and work on his part.

Sid's mother tried to hide her disappointment, though Sid guessed she'd been hoping he'd go out for pizza or something with them. But Sid wasn't disappointed, she was suspicious.

She was even more so after a hurried conversation with Joel one day before school.

"Hey, Sid," he said, coming up to where she was struggling with her locker combination. "Can I talk to you a minute?" The two walked to an isolated alcove housing a broken drinking fountain.

Joel coughed and looked down at his shoes. "I overheard some girls gossiping yesterday. I usually don't pay attention, but . . . well, they were saying that your Mom's been dating Byron Vincenti?"

Sid flushed angrily. "What business is it of theirs who my mom dates? She's old enough!"

"Sure. Hey don't get mad. It's just that, well, with what we've been piecing together about Byron, it seems that, well, maybe that's not a good idea."

"Of course it's not! It's a lousy idea! But what can I do about it? I can't exactly go along as chaperon. I can't even warn her. She wouldn't believe me. I mean it really sounds like something out of a third-rate horror movie."

She fidgeted angrily with the locket at her throat, then looked up at him. "Joel, I'm so worried! Suppose he tries to get her to join his coven or whatever, or drink blood or something?"

Awkwardly Joel patted her arm. "It's probably nothing like that, Sid. We're both crazy to give it a thought. It's just that . . . well, the other night after the show I stayed around to reset my lights, and Byron almost threw me out, accusing me of hanging around to spy on him."

"Oh."

"And you know what that sounds like?"

"Yes. Like there is something to spy on."

A conspiratorial smile played about his lips. "Should we?"

She grinned back. "Let's talk at lunch."

Plans were laid, and on the night of the second to the last show, Sid suggested to her mother that they leave right afterward instead of staying to help as usual. Mrs. Guthrie agreed. Seven evenings and one matinee as Rose Maybud had somewhat tried her enthusiasm. Once home they went directly to bed, foregoing their usual chat over toast and cocoa.

Sid was tired. But a bubbling combination of fear and excitement kept her eyes open as she sat in bed fully dressed. Beside her, the luminous hands of her clock scarcely moved. She tried to picture what might be waiting for them at the theater, but that gave her acute stage fright, so she forced her thoughts in different directions.

What happened in the hall at school yesterday—that was something to think about! She started getting mad all over again. She'd been minding her own business, walking to class, when suddenly she heard her name. Viola Nolton and her friend Stephanie were walking in front and talking about *her*. It had made her so mad she could remember almost every word.

"Of course, Sid Guthrie wants to be president of the school drama club," Viola stated. (It wasn't true, she didn't want to be. It'd be fun, but would take too much time.) "She and her mother think they can just move into town and start *running* things. Just because Mrs. Guthrie's got a loud voice and big blue eyes, she expects to get *all* the lead roles and tie *all* the eligible men in knots."

"Well," Stephanie commented, "at least Sid doesn't take after her there."

Viola snickered. "Just let her *try* running for club president; the only vote she'll get will be her own. It takes more than grades. *Looks* count for something there, you know. Lord, the only makeup she ever wears is onstage."

"The only *boys* she ever touches are onstage." Stephanie added as the two stood for a moment, and Sid hid behind a bank of lockers. "*Except* maybe for that overgrown grasshopper, Joel Griggins, who *lights* the stage. What a pair of nerds. They *deserve* each other."

Sid was still seething. She wished she had done something besides hide until the others had left. She wished she'd stomped right up and said something scathing and witty. She could think of all kinds of things now, like, "Well, at least I don't go onstage just so people can ogle me," or "Some people can make friends without plastering themselves with makeup." Not very good. How about, "At least Joel Griggins doesn't . . ."

Suddenly she remembered. She looked at the clock. Somehow an hour had passed. Time to go.

Before anger could slide totally back into fear, she hopped out of bed, grabbed her flashlight from the bedside table, and began easing open the back window. She fumbled for the stick to prop it up. Then pulling on her parka, which she'd hung over a bedpost, she crawled awkwardly onto the kitchen roof.

She'd done this a few times when they'd first moved in. It seemed the adventruous sort of thing to do in an old house—sort of Tom Sawyerish. When her mother had objected, she'd said she needed to practice escape routes in case of fire.

The difficulty was, however, to get quietly from the kitchen roof to the shed and then to the ground. She supposed it wouldn't matter how much noise you made if there really were a fire. There'd be flames crackling and sirens and all. But now she was trying for stealth.

Gingerly she lowered herself onto the top of the shed, and promptly several boards screeched. She froze, half on, half off the roof. But really, she told herself, the wind was making more noise than that just rattling shingles and slamming the shed door. Good old wind.

She eased herself down, ignoring the continued creaking. From the shed she stepped to the sawhorse standing beside the wall. It wobbled alarmingly, but she jumped to the ground before it could throw her there. She cast a quick look back to the house. No lights on. Before second thoughts could hit, she scurried off into the night.

There was no snow tonight, only cold. The wind blew as steadily and loudly as a train, whipping the cold right through her and pushing her along from behind. Above, it roared through the black trees as if it wanted to get somewhere, too.

But when Sid reached the darkened theater, she wasn't at all sure she wanted to be there. There was no turning back, though. Joel was clearly there already: the door was propped open for her. She slipped inside, closing the door after her.

It was dark inside, pitch dark, and she didn't dare switch

on a light. Slowly she walked through the open space, her arms outstretched like someone playing Helen Keller. But she wasn't thinking about that play. She was thinking about the other things that might move into the dark space. Dark themselves, and cold.

She almost screamed when her fingers grazed against the far wall. Her hands slid over the framed pictures. Was one of them that ghostly picture of Hamlet? She swallowed and moved on, around the corner and down the corridor. The wood paneling gave way to a cold metal door. She found the knob and turned it.

The space inside felt close and small. She groped for the metal stairs and crawled up them on all fours like a cat. She tried to think light as a cat, but the metal groaned and complained just the same.

She was almost at the top when Joel's voice whispered out of the darkness above her. "The others have just left, but Byron's still here."

"What's he doing?"

"Nothing. Just sitting on the stage."

The two crouched together in the cramped little space listening to the wind grate over the roof. The darkness around them smelled of hot dust and wiring. Sid leaned back against the cold knobby base of the cannonlike follow spot. It was awfully crowded on the floor of the light booth. She refused to think about Viola's innuendos.

"Joel," she whispered, "what do we do if we find out . . . well, if he *is* a witch?"

"Warlock."

"Huh?"

"Warlock, male witch. Well, we could denounce him and have a trial."

"No!"

"Shhh! I was joking."

After a silence she whispered, "Well, maybe if we

confront him with it, he'll stop doing . . . whatever he's doing."

"Maybe. And if he is making those things appear, he'd better stop soon."

"Why *soon?*" she asked.

"Because I doubt that we two or George are especially psychic or observant, yet we've seen them. If more people, responsible types, start seeing them and words gets out— well, it wouldn't do the theater any good."

"I hadn't thought of that. I guess there's a difference between having a reputedly haunted theater and having a confirmed one."

"Right."

Silence. Then faint noises from the distant stage. "What's he doing now?" Sid asked.

Joel got on his knees. "He's got the stage work lights on, and he's walking around doing something. I can't tell what."

"Can we get any closer?"

"We can crawl along the catwalk from here to the stage. Then if we stay down flat, maybe we can see. But we'll have to be awfully quiet."

By now, Sid was up on her knees too, looking out over the empty seats to the dimly lit stage. "Let's try. He's doing something on the stage floor, and I can't make it out."

Cautiously, they opened the door from the light booth to the catwalk, and on hands and knees crawled along its dark uncomfortable length. When they'd passed beyond the proscenium arch to the backstage area, the concealing waist-high wall gave way to two metal rails. They got down on their stomachs and inched along like commandos. Positioning themselves between two of the black side curtains, they peered over the edge at the scene below.

Sid didn't know what she'd expected. A bubbling

cauldron? Vats of newt eyes? Whatever, she hadn't expected to see Byron Vincenti playing with chalk.

Wearing jeans and a black sweater, the actor was working on hands and knees, drawing things on the stage floor. From above, it looked like a huge star with strange squiggles in the points.

Wavering columns of incense were rising from somewhere below. The sharp cloying smell tickled Sid's nose. She hoped she wouldn't sneeze. Surely that only happened in corny movies.

At last the man stood up and surveyed his handiwork. Apparently satisfied, he walked to someplace out of sight and returned holding two candles, black ones, in a pair of silver candlesticks. He carefully placed one on each side of the chalk figure and lit them with a cigarette lighter.

As Sid lay there, a thought crept over her. It was fairly dark where they were hiding, but suppose Byron chanced to look up and see them? What might he do? Turn them into toads? Suddenly she did not want to be there. But now she was afraid to move.

Again Byron left their range of vision and returned holding a thick book in what looked like library binding. He opened it to a place marked with an old envelope, then frowning he flipped to another marked spot and began reading out something that sounded like Latin. Sid wasn't sure, but she didn't think his pronunciation was very good.

Repeating the same phrase over and over again, he walked slowly around the chalked figure. When he was back where he'd started, he consulted another page, then walked off again to return with what looked like a bottle of wine.

Deliberately, he stepped on one of the star's tips and in his rich baritone voice began chanting something else Latinish, his eyes fixed all the while on the book. Sid got the feeling that if Byron was a witch, or warlock, he was a student one. He didn't seem too sure about whatever he was doing.

Nonetheless, something appeared to be happening. The shadows on the far side of the stage looked thicker than before. Darkness seemed to coil around the bases of walls and curtains like rolls of sooty dust. She squinted against the light but could make out no shapes, just a dark billowing presence. She glanced to where Joel lay on his stomach a few feet to her right. He nodded. He had noticed it too.

But if Byron was aware of the new presence, he ignored it. Now he squatted down, and after struggling to pull the cork from the bottle, he poured a puddle of wine inside one point of the star. With a finger he traced it into a damp red pattern, stopping occasionally for a non-Latin sounding curse, or to consult illustrations in the book.

He repeated this at each point until he had worked around to where Sid couldn't see him. Cautiously, she inched forward and peered further over the edge.

At last, having completed the circuit, he moved altogether out of sight, and they could hear him rummaging through something. Sid edged further forward and found that by leaning out and gripping an edge of a curtain, she could angle herself around and see what was happening under the catwalk.

Byron was squatting down and sorting impatiently through a large box. Patches of darkness seemed to be forming on this side of the stage as well. One was taking shape.

Sid's mouth went dry. She had seen this one before. The shadow was becoming the turbaned black man, and in one upraised hand he held a dagger.

She wanted to scream. The wraith, still swimming in and out of focus, was floating several feet above the stage floor. But it was floating toward Byron, who was still busily digging through the box. Sid drew her breath to warn him, but just then he looked up.

Instead of jumping back, flinching from the dagger, he swept an arm at the figure as one might at a bothersome dog. The thing curled away like a plume of smoke, losing itself in the folds of a curtain. Sid wriggled out further to see what had become of it.

Just then, Byron yelled, "Ah, ha!" pulling a small box from the litter. Sid jerked and pulled back suddenly. The curtain she was clinging to ripped. She overbalanced and with a squeal, began slipping over the edge. Joel grabbed at her leg. She flipped over, and it twisted out of his grasp.

Flailing wildly, she swung out onto the curtain, clutching at it with her other hand. Everything seemed to happen in slow motion. Slowly she slid down the folds of the black curtain. Slowly the old frabric ripped above her. A picture flashed into her mind from some old movie of a swashbuckling hero swinging dashingly down a curtain. She felt far from dashing.

Abruptly, the curtain ripped free. She dropped the last few feet. Yards of black material billowed down on top of her.

Everything was silent, dusty, and dark. Then through her black shroud, she heard footsteps. She was too shaken to even try to get away.

A hand gripped the material around her and yanked it off. The dark eyes staring down at her blazed with anger.

CHAPTER

Sid sat amid the ruined curtain, gazing up at Byron Vincenti's furious, almost demented face. He's going to turn me into a toad, she thought. But the adrenaline was still pumping through her from the fall. Clenching her fists, she rose shakily to her feet. She wouldn't take it sitting down!

"What are you doing here?" Byron's voice was icy.

The best defense is an offense, she thought crazily, kicking her way free of the old curtain. "We . . . I've been watching you, Byron." It seemed best to keep the reserves secret. "I know what you're doing. You're a witch, a warlock. You've been conjuring up spirits to haunt this place. I don't know why. But I can tell you . . . you'd just better stop it!"

She yelled the last, trying to make up in volume for the lack in content.

Byron stood staring at her, opening and closing his mouth, as if unable to decide what curse to throw at her. Then to her utter surprise, he threw his hands over his face and seemed to crumple in on himself. Sagging to his knees, he broke into sobs.

Now it was Sid's turn to stand with open mouth. "What . . . ? Hey, Byron, I'm sorry. I only meant to . . ."

Not looking up, he waved her off. His voice was thick and choked. "It doesn't matter. Just go away. Leave me alone."

"But . . ."

"Go away! It's no good. Just leave me alone with these husks. Go!"

Sid glanced up at the catwalk, fifteen feet above. Joel, his eyes wide, was crouching in the shadows. She saw that he was clinging to a curtain rope, obviously meaning to swing down if she needed him. Maybe he'd make a more convincing swashbuckler.

Confused, she looked at Byron again, his huddled body still convulsed with sobs. Slowly she backed away, then looked quickly behind her. No misty figures lurked in the shadows. She turned and began walking swiftly across the stage. The only sound was her footsteps and the wind howling outside. No incantations, no whispering shadows. Maybe she wouldn't become a toad.

She had almost reached the steps when Byron unfolded himself and thrust a shaking finger toward her. "No! Don't go! If you go, you'll tell everyone, you'll tell your mother. Then I'll be finished here, and I'm not ready. Not yet!"

Sid turned and looked back at him, but kept inching toward the steps.

Byron staggered to his feet, raking a hand through his tousled black hair. "Wait, please wait. Let me explain. Maybe if you understand, you'll keep quiet. I don't want to leave here."

Sid didn't move, curiosity vying with fear. She didn't dare glance up, but hoped that Joel was ready to do his Douglas Fairbanks bit if Byron suddenly whipped out a magic wand.

But the man just stood there, looking dejectedly down at his chalk drawings. Suddenly angry, he scuffed them away with his foot. "It's no good! I've tried and tried, but it'll never work. Someone like me can never make it work!"

He looked up, and Sid was startled at the pain and sorrow seaming his face. He didn't seem to be acting.

"Don't you see? I wasn't trying to call up spirits, I was trying to get rid of them! I've read up on it and I have all the right words and gadgets, but it never works. And I know why, too. I keep trying, hoping I'm wrong. But I'm not!"

He laughed bitterly, pacing across the stage. Then he spun around toward her. "They aren't real spirits, you see. Not lost tormented souls. They *haven't* any souls. None! No more than I have. That's why I can't work magic, I guess. No soul! Oh, he's well and truly trapped me. No way out!"

Sid decided he was not a warlock. Just mad, raving mad. Some improvement! She began again inching her way back toward the stairs.

Byron looked at her, his tormented expression slowly softening. "Sorry. I should be more coherent or you'll think I'm just crazy. Though it's nearly driven me that way. Sit down, why don't you."

Almost on their own, her legs folded under her and she sat on the worn floorboards. Byron paced back and forth across center stage.

"I'm not nearly as young as I look. I'm trapped, you see. I don't even age without a soul. But if I could have it back I'd gladly grow old or die tomorrow—anything instead of this living nothing!"

He laughed again, a dry brittle sound. "I used to think that theater was the only life worth living. I grew up in New York and hung around theaters from the time I was a kid. My father wanted me to be a lawyer; he said I was cantankerous and pigheaded enough for one; but all I wanted to do was act. I hung around backstage, watching, running errands. I'll never forget the first time I saw Edwin

Booth. I wanted more than anything to act like that, to get parts like his."

"Edwin Booth?" Sid said shakily.

"Yes, that was in the fifties, the 1850s. He was a stupendous actor. But it was his crazy brother who won all the immortality. Ha! What a travesty!"

Sid just swallowed and said nothing.

"I was around so much, I started getting bit parts. But nothing big. Maybe a few lines if I was lucky, like 'General, your horse is ready.'

"It made me furious. I knew I had talent, but I never got a chance to show it. Then one day in a rage after a rehearsal I shouted, 'I'd give up my soul for lead parts!' The next day . . . the offer was accepted."

Byron turned and seemed to stare right through her at a scene only he could see. "It was after a performance of *Julius Ceasar*. I was still in my soldier's costume brooding backstage about how I'd be a spear carrier the rest of my days. This fellow in black and red with a great plumed hat came up to me. He called me by name and swirled his cape in a deep bow." Byron imitated the sweeping gesture.

"He said, 'My apologies for this rather theatrical costume. Generally theater people expect me to look like something from Faust.' His forked goatee quivered as he laughed."

Byron clamped his hands to his head. "That laugh! You'll think I was crazy to believe him when he said he was the Devil. But there was no doubt. Evil rose from him like smoke from a fire.

"He looked me in the eye. 'You offered to sell me your soul, sir, in exchange for lead parts. I have come to finalize that deal.'"

As Byron talked and moved, Sid could almost see the scene.

"I was crazy with fear. But my father was right, I should

71

have been a lawyer. 'No,' I said, pretending calm. 'I did not say I would *sell* my soul, and I never mentioned *you*. I only offered to *give it up*. That is a very different thing.'

"He snarled at me. 'Oh, is it? You damned squirming barrister, we'll see about that!' He pulled a smoking paper from this pocket and thrust it at me. 'This is a standard contract. Sign it, and we have an agreement. So many years of leads for you, and, eventually, your soul for me.'

"I shook my head, and he smiled dreadfully. 'If you wish to stick to your petty legalisms, then do so by all means. Give up your soul. Send it into limbo—out of my hands, and out of yours. See what it's like to live with no one's claim on you—not mine, not even your own.' He laughed again like a dying crow.

"He jiggled the paper before me. 'Now sign!' I hated him. I wanted more than anything to defeat him. 'No,' I shouted and spat on his paper. It sizzled like a skillet.

"And like hot coals, his eyes glowed at me. 'All right, then! The suggestion was yours. Try the other, try living without a soul. But sooner or later, young man, you'll change your mind, you'll beg me for a deal.' He laughed again. 'Sooner, I think—much, much sooner!' There was incredible light and sound, and I felt as if I'd been axed in two.

"Everyone thought lightning had struck the theater. When I came to, I felt all empty, like a hollow shell going through the motions of breathing and talking. As days went by, I could almost feel myself fading, thinning into nothing!"

The actor stopped pacing and slumped to the floor of the stage. "You have no idea how scared I was. But I was mad, too. I wouldn't let that snake win! Maybe I didn't have my soul, but neither did he. I wouldn't sell it to him now for all the leads in theater. Let it stay in limbo. I'd just learn to live without a soul!

"In despair, I really threw myself into acting. I was at the theater twenty hours a day, taking any part I could get and putting everything into it. Pretty soon directors noticed and started giving me better roles. I lived for those roles— literally. I began to see that when I totally became a stage character, I sort of borrowed a soul. I gave the character a body and it gave me a kind of inner substance; I stopped fading. When the run of the play ended, though, it started again."

Byron stood up. "It was a stalemate, you see. Despite him, I managed to hang on to some sort of life. I didn't have to beg him for a deal. But I was trapped just the same."

He laughed wryly. "It made me a good actor, though. I got better and better roles. And it was because of *my* work, not his. But I acted now not for love of the stage, but to foil the Devil. And I knew that if I ever gave up and stopped acting, without a soul, I'd just fade away. No proper death with Heaven or Hell waiting. Trapped in limbo, my soul would face eternal emptiness. Nothing!"

Spinning around, he pointed wildly at the curtains and the smoky wraith of a man floating there. "Nothing! Like I see in their eyes! Would that they *were* ghosts, honest lost souls. But no, they're only empty shells, discarded husks of characters I've played. The fake souls I somehow gave life to while trying to eke out my own life.

"It's weird, you know, but I used to wonder about them—how I with no soul could possibly create these shadowy creatures. But you see, it's the intensity. It creates these shadows, these enduring reflections. I guess all great actors do it—perhaps that's why there are so many 'haunted' theaters. But other actors leave just faint traces because they lack the intensity of my need. They have souls and lives of their own to go back to.

"Even these creations of mine fade eventually. But too slowly. After a while a theater gets full of them. People start to notice, and I have to move on. I change my name and find some sort of job in a new town where there's a theater small enough for me to get parts but not much outside notice. But it's awkward, after a while, not seeming to age. I have to put a lot of distance between one stop and the next so one recognizes me. I've been *here* before, actually, around the turn of the century."

He turned and began pacing vigorously. "But this time I hoped I could get rid of these things some other way. I don't want to leave here. I'm so tired, so tired of moving about, so tired of hiding. And I like the people here. I like your mother, though I know I could never be close with her." He sighed. "I can never be close with anyone. But at least let me stay somewhere peaceful a little longer."

Suddenly he swooped down on Sid. Grabbing her shoulders, he pulled her to her feet. "Don't tell them. Please don't tell them! They'll think I'm mad or in league with the Devil. Either way, they'll drive me out!"

"Hey, stop that!" a quavery voice yelled from above. "Leave her alone!" With a yelp and a creaking of rope, Joel swooped down to land sprawling on the stage a few feet away.

"Two of you!" Byron spun around as Joel staggered to his feet. But slowly the man's anger seemed to drain out of him, leaving him drooped and sad. "And I suppose that now *you* will tell."

"I won't. Not if you don't hurt her."

Byron hung his head. "I won't hurt her, or you—or anyone. That way he'd win, too. If I resort to evil, I'll forfeit my soul as surely as if I'd signed his wretched papers. No, if I must, I'll go on as I am—an eternally defiant fool! Better that than eternal damnation, or eternal nothing."

He strode over to a chair where he'd thrown his cape and swirled it around his shoulders. "But what have I ahead?

74

An eternity of empty playacting, pursued by meddlesome mortals and empty mocking specters!"

As he strode off across the stage, Joel whispered with shaky bravado. "A little theatrical, isn't he?"

The retreating figure spun around. "Of course, I'm theatrical! That's all that's left for me!" He turned, leaped off the stage, and, running up the aisle, burst through the side door. Darkness engulfed him as the wind howled through the open door.

Alone on the stage, Sid and Joel shivered, though not from the cold. The wind snuffed out the black candles and buffeted dark misty shadows about the stage. As one whirled past, Sid caught a glimpse of eyes, great black hollows opening onto nothing.

CHAPTER

Joel and Sid said little to each other about what had happened. It wasn't ready for words yet. But Sid certainly thought about it. She tried not to. The whole thing was so disturbing, so abnormal that remembering made her feel all creepy and confused.

By showtime the next night, the last night of the play, she was so troubled, she doubted she could stay in character. How could you be a giggling, mindless village bridesmaid when you were wondering if the leading man would suddenly vanish in a puff of smoke.

From offstage she watched the ghost scene extra carefully, half expecting their regular ghostly chorus to be joined by irregulars as they tormented poor Ruthven Murgatroyd.

But nothing happened except that, if anything, Byron Vincenti played his role better than ever, putting everything he had into it. Or rather, she realized, taking everything he could out of it.

By the next day, she had decided not to let this thing get to her. They'd had a fun cast party after the final show, and this morning she and her mother were going to church.

She sat beside her mother on the hard wooden pew and tried to concentrate on what Rev. Aikens was saying. If ever she needed spiritual uplifting, she thought, it was now. He was preaching from the book of James, about how the only thing God wants of people is that they help one another. She wondered if that applied to people without souls. Byron certainly needed help, though how anyone might provide it, she couldn't imagine.

Rev. Aikens's words rolled on and on, and soon her eyes drifted to the stained-glass window. Christ looked rather limp and pale standing amid all those folks in brilliant blues and reds. The sun glowing through that colored glass, gave her a feeling of being safe and happy in the heart of a jewel.

She wondered why Christ was always so wimpy looking in pictures. He couldn't have been like that. He'd caused a lot of trouble in his time, really rocked the boat. Just as Dennis Aikens was doing now in this town with all of his talk about God's call to social action and involvement. It wasn't what this congregation was used to. They probably would have preferred a minister more like one in *The Crucible*. Or maybe that old local minister whose books Rev. Aikens had found. Real hellfire types.

Something jabbed her in the ribs. With a start she realized the sermon was over and they were passing the collection plate. Guiltily she dropped in her quarter, sweaty and warm from being clutched in her hand, then quickly passed the plate to her mother. Now everyone in church would know she'd been daydreaming. But she didn't care. She had the spark of an idea.

Sid could barely hide her impatience during lunch. When she got an idea, she liked to act on it right away. Even little delays made her itchy.

Finally, while her mother cleared the table, Sid slipped away to the shop and the old bookcase. She stopped and stared. Half the shelves were bare, the gaps filled with plaster gnomes. With withering hope, she ran a finger over the spines of the remaining books. But it was gone.

That old book that Rev. Aikens had brought in, the one

about how to handle the supernatural. It might have been just what she needed. And now some tourist had probably bought it, taking it off to Louisville or somewhere.

A few minutes later when her mother came to open the shop, she found Sid on her knees staring at the bookshelf with a vacant expression.

"What's up?" Mrs. Guthrie asked. "You look like you've lost your last friend."

Sid started. "No, only a book. What happened to . . . to all those books you had here?"

"The books?" Her mother thought a moment as she flipped the window sign from "Closed, Call Again" to "Open." "Well, a young couple came in last week and bought that thirty-dollar volume of hunting prints. Kind of a horsy-looking pair. I bet they're going to cut out all the horse prints and spend three hundred dollars having them framed."

"Yes, but the other books?"

"Is this a spot inventory?"

"Oh, it's just that one of them looked kind of interesting. And I thought that, if I were careful and all, I'd like to look at it."

"Sure, no problem as long as you're careful."

Mrs. Guthrie took a dust rag to one of the glass cases. "Now, let's see. I sold an old romance novel to some woman from Gentryville. But actually I think most of those books went to Karl Johansen about three week ago. He's a rare book collector, you know. Claire says he's got a couple of rooms practically lined with them."

"Mr. Johansen!" Sid jumped up. "Thanks, Mom!" She rushed out the door and was past the gate before the little bells stopped jangling.

Sid ran most of the four blocks to Becky's house, but slowed as she came in sight of it. A sheet of cardboard on the lawn proclaimed "Yard Sale" in large uneven letters.

She'd forgotten about the sale. Becky had said they'd have one this weekend if it wasn't too cold. Sid wondered if there was anything good left. She loved yard sales; other people's junk was always interesting.

Then an awful thought struck her. Suppose Becky's dad had lost interest in that book and decided to sell it? Who knows where it could be now?

Sid hurried into the yard, stopping at a card table piled with books. A stack of paperback romances—Becky's mom read those by the carload—and some animal books that even Becky's little brother had outgrown. There were also some *National Geographics* and cookbooks. But nothing that looked like a batch of rare volumes.

Louisa, Becky's big sister, was the only Johansen in the yard. She was looking at Sid. "You here to see Becky?"

"Uh, yeah."

"She's rummaging through her room to see if she can part with anything else. Go on in."

Sid dashed through the familiar route to her friend's bedroom, and found the back half of Becky sticking out from under the bed.

"Hi, Becky."

"Yow!" Startled, Becky bumped her head on the slats of the bed. She squirmed out backward.

"Warn a person, will you?" She sat up rubbing her head.

"Sorry. Finding anything more for the sale?"

"Not much. Just this ball the dog's chewed and a doll that was on my birthday cake a couple of years ago. She's in pretty good shape, except for a missing foot."

Sid sat down on the bed. "Has your dad given any of his books to the sale?"

"Are you kidding? He'd rather sell us."

"Good. Not about selling you—I mean . . . you see, I think my mom sold him a book that I kind of need myself." Sid floundered for a moment then brightened with an idea.

"You see, I wanted to give it to Byron Vincenti. It's about supernatural stuff, and that's . . . that's sort of a hobby of Byron's."

Sid saw her friend's face light up at the mention of her idol. "Ooh, to think you know him well enough to know about his hobbies! But did I tell you the Smiths down the street hired him to do some repairs on their porch. I got to see him there all day yesterday! Isn't that unbearable?"

"Yeah, terrific." Sid felt like a heel. But then in a way, this really was for Byron. "So, about the book. You don't suppose your dad would consider maybe selling it back . . . to me, that is? I mean, I don't know how rare it is or anything. But I bet Byron sure would like it."

Becky stood up, a resolute look on her plump face. "I'll ask him. He may bite my head off, but I'll die in a good cause."

Sid told her what she could remember of the title, and her friend bravely marched out of the room. Sid waited on the bed, looking idly at Becky's doll collection. She hoped that book wasn't too valuable. She didn't want to sink half a year's allowance into it. This scheme was just beginning to jell in her mind, and the more shape it took, the more harebrained it seemed.

A few minutes later, Becky burst into the room, clutching a large leather-bound volume to her chest. "Here, it's yours . . . it's *his!* Dad said he discovered it wasn't a first edition after all. And since you're a special friend and all . . . you can have it."

Sid swallowed. "What do I owe him?"

"Nothing! He said just be sure you buy something at the yard sale."

Half an hour later, Sid headed home with a grocery bag holding the precious book, a dog-chewed ball, and a couple of 25¢ Indian bead necklaces. Once home she threw the ball to a highly uninterested Fred, then ran upstairs to drop the necklaces in her jewelry box and stuff the book in its bag under her bed.

It took her a long time to get to sleep that night. Half-formed plans floated in her mind and kept colliding with guilt over deceiving Becky. But her friend turned pale at even the mildest ghost stories, and she'd probably faint if she heard the truth about her theatrical heartthrob.

What made Sid even more restless was the book itself. She could almost feel it lying there, crouching there, under her bed. She didn't really know what sort of strangeness it had between its covers, but she suspected it was stuff that, if she were being sensible, she'd leave alone. The sooner she got this plan underway and that book out of her room, the better.

The next day at school as they passed between classes, she asked Joel to come over after dinner. Something important relating to you-know-who. Joel nodded.

When Sid told her mother about Joel coming to work on homework that night, she only nodded and said, "Fine dear. Now, would you do me the favor of vacuuming the parlor while I finish with this banana bread?"

"But, Mom, it's only Joel? He . . ."

"Oh, ye of little memory. Have you forgotten that tonight's our turn to host the Blake Theater board meeting?"

Sid swallowed and hurried in search of the vacuum cleaner. Well, at least there'd be something to divert her mother while she and Joel plotted.

Joel was the first to appear, and he and Sid were established in the dining room with schoolbooks spread over the table before the board members began arriving. The two paid studious attention to their books until Mrs. Guthrie had finished bustling back and forth between kitchen and parlor with coffee and banana bread.

When the meeting was well underway in the other room, Sid slipped upstairs and returned with the book still wrapped in its grocery bag.

She plopped it on the table like something dead. "I'll be glad to have the thing out of my room. I kept dreaming about unclean spirits rising out of it and doing all sorts of nastiness. Here, let's open it on these newspapers. The binding's decaying and makes an awful mess."

When the big volume lay before them, Joel reverently blew dust off its cover. "Do you really think there'll be something here we can use?"

"I don't know. But there ought to be. It says it covers 'all manner of supernatural dealings,' or something like that."

"Well, I agree, we ought to try to help Byron somehow. I mean, he's certainly in trouble, to say nothing of the trouble we're all in if that theater keeps filling up with his old character ghosts or whatever. Just think, there's probably a Ruthven Murgatroyd ghost flitting around here right now."

Sid shivered. "That must be why he starts learning new parts so soon, even before tryouts. He has to become some new character, just to stay alive."

"Yeah, that's creepy," Joel said. "Like a vampire having to drink blood, or something." This time they both shivered.

Joel cleared his throat and turned to the book's elaborate table of contents. "Let's get down to business before we freak each other out."

"There's a section here on detecting witches," Sid pointed out. "But that's no good. We already know he's not a witch, though not from want of trying, it seems. I didn't know you have to have a soul to work magic, but then I guess I never *really* believed in magic."

Joel ran his finger down a page. "Well, what about this, 'The Exorcism of Ghosts and Other Lost Souls'?"

"No good. Those things don't have souls."

They turned a page. After a moment, Sid tapped an entry. "What about this: 'On Matters Dealing with Compacts with the Devil'? Page three sixty-four."

"Sounds good."

Turning the fragile pages carefully, they pored over spell after spell, all written in archaic language. Finally Joel leaned back and ran a hand through his hair.

"This is all terrific stuff, but it's rather specialized. A how-to book for professionals."

Sid nodded. "Rev. Aikens said something about its being meant for ordained ministers. Now I see what he meant. It sounds like you'll be zapped if you try to do this stuff and aren't a clergyman."

"Or clergywoman."

"I don't think they had those then."

"Well," Joel continued after a moment, "do you think your Rev. Aikens could be persuaded to perform one of these things himself?"

Sid sighed. "I doubt it. He's an awfully twentieth-century sort of minister. He probably doesn't even believe in this stuff." She patted the book dejectedly then quickly covered it with a notebook as she heard someone coming from the parlor.

Mrs. Guthrie, carrying a coffeepot, was followed by Mrs. Nolton with an empty platter.

"*Honestly*, Amelia," Mrs. Nolton was saying, "I just don't know *what* to do. We sent for those *Devil and Daniel Webster* scripts *ages* ago. And *what* just came in the mail? Twenty copies of *Arsenic and Old Lace!*"

"Well, that's a nice enough play," Mrs. Guthrie said amiably. "We could do that instead."

"*Honestly*, my dear! We couldn't *possibly*. The whole season's already been *advertised*. And besides, such a *newcomer* as yourself wouldn't know, but we did *Arsenic* five years ago. It wouldn't *do* to repeat so soon, my dear.

But I just don't know *what* to do. All we have is one typewritten copy of the script from years back, and tryouts are *Thursday*."

"Well," Mrs. Guthrie suggested, "I suppose we could Xerox that script."

"My dear, we couldn't *possibly!* That would be against copyright." She paused thoughtfully for a moment. "Though, I suppose . . . since we did order and *pay* for the right ones, and *they* sent us the wrong ones . . . Well, it really wouldn't be right, but it *was* their fault and time *is* short. I suppose we could Xerox, just this once. Yes. Yes, that's really a very *resourceful* idea of yours, Amelia. I'll leave you the script. Could you have twenty-five copies ready by Thursday?"

"Er, well, yes, Dahlia, I suppose I could."

The two women passed back through the dining room with refilled coffeepot and platter. Sid buried her face in a book so they couldn't see the devious smile that had spread over it.

But Joel had seen. "Hey, what is it?" he whispered when the others were gone. "You look positively demonic."

Looking across the table at him, she lowered her voice dramatically. "I just got an absolutely ingenious idea."

"What is it?"

"Do you type?"

"Type? Well, sort of. Why?"

"Because we're going to do a little selective editing of Stephen Vincent Benét's classic American play."

Until it was time for Joel to go home, the two huddled around the dining room table like generals around a battle map. Pieces of an audacious plan were beginning to fall into place, but everything depended on Sid's succeeding in the next step.

She had her doubts about that particular operation, but

the next day after school she resolutely launched into it. When, following a slower than usual walk, she actually reached the door of the church office, she was hit with second thoughts. Fighting them down, she turned the knob and walked in.

The prim-looking secretary raised her eyes from her typewriter and smiled blandly. "May I help you, young lady?"

"Yes, I need to see Rev. Aikens if he's not too busy. It's . . . kind of important."

"Just a minute. Sidonie Guthrie, isn't it? Just sit over there please." The elderly woman got up and disappeared into another office.

Nervously, Sid perched on the edge of the couch. She felt as if she were waiting to see the principal. Maybe this wasn't such a good idea. Maybe she should just slip out the door and . . .

The secretary returned. "Rev. Aikens will see you now." She smiled and ushered Sid into a small book-lined office.

Dennis Aikens stood up with a warm, slightly puzzled smile on his face. "Sit down, Sidonie, sit down. Now what is it you want to talk with me about?"

Oh brother, she thought, he probably thinks I'm here to unburden my troubled soul. Maybe I'm a despairing teenager comtemplating suicide. Too bad it's nothing that simple.

"Well, Rev. Aikens, it's like this. You have a problem, and we have a problem. So maybe we can help each other out."

His smile, beneath his bushy mustache, now looked bemused. "All right. What are our respective problems?"

"Well, clearly you're having trouble fitting in here."

Now he looked startled.

"We did, too, when we first came. These are really tight

little communities, these southern Indiana towns. They're hard to break into and be accepted."

He laughed rather self-consciously. "Well, that's a pretty fair analysis. Have you thought of going into sociology?"

Sid blushed but forged ahead. "What we did was start getting involved in community things. It broke down barriers, sort of."

"Well, actually, Sidonie, I have been working on that sort of thing. I've started up several interest groups in the congregation already. People are a little slow to get involved, but we're making headway."

"That's fine. But it's not really what I meant. You need to get into something outside the church so people can see you in a new light, as part of the community. We did it with theater, and I bet that would work for you, too. After going through a production together, everyone feels like part of a team."

"Goodness, Sidonie!" He laughed. "I haven't acted since high school."

"That doesn't matter. We're all amateurs. Besides, you have lots of experience. Acting's sort of like preaching. You have a good strong voice. And then you have one real advantage—you're a man. We're always short on men, and most plays have more men's parts than women's."

He looked vaguely thoughtful, and Sid jumped in again before he could put her off.

"We're doing *The Devil and Daniel Webster* next, and we need a good Daniel Webster. It's a terrific part for you. You'd get to best the Devil. And that has to be great public relations for a minister. The old ladies in this church always come to see our plays. And if they see you in that part, they're sure to get all swoony and think of you as a really heroic sort of guy. It'd be terrific for business."

The minister was grinning now. "Maybe you should be an ad executive. You're pretty convincing."

"Oh good! We really need you. And you're always saying how one should help the needy." She stood up before she went overboard on this. "The tryouts are this Thursday night at the theater. Seven o'clock. I'm counting on seeing you there, now."

As she walked away from the church, it was Sid's turn to look bemused. She couldn't believe she had actually done that. What gall! Walk right into a minister's office and badger him into something, and with ulterior motives, too.

She wondered if that was some sort of sin. No, she shook her head. No, this was definitely a good cause. But it did look as if theater training had its uses. She never could have done that a couple of years ago. She was afraid, however, that now it was going to take a lot more than acting to pull this off.

CHAPTER

10

All day Thursday, Sid was tingling with excitement, but when school finally came to an end, she still had to keep it hidden. She didn't want her mother wondering why she was so worked up over this particular tryout. Somehow she just had to get through the hours until seven o'clock.

She couldn't keep her mind on homework, so she offered to help with dinner. Standing over the kitchen sink, she poured a basket of cherry tomatoes into a colander and began washing them one by one.

"You know, Sidonie," her mother said as she was cutting carrots. "I'm thinking maybe we shouldn't try out for this play."

Sid squeezed a tomato so hard it popped across the room and disappeared behind the stove.

"Why not?" she gasped. "Oh, Mom, it's a great play. You don't want to miss out on this one."

"Well, these plays take so much time. Besides, I've had my share of big parts this year. And . . . and I really don't want to play Mary, Jabez Stone's wife. Not with the way the casting's likely to go, I guess."

Ah, so that was it, Sid realized. Byron Vincenti would probably get the part of Jabez Stone, and her mother didn't want to play opposite him. Sid could certainly understand that, now more than ever. But it was absolutely essential that they, or she at least, be in this play.

"You wouldn't have to try out for the lead," she said desperately. "There are plenty of smaller parts."

"Oh, I don't know, maybe it's better to just sit this one out."

Sid decided to lay on the guilt trip. "But, Mom, it's such a fun play. And you know they don't let kids in a show unless a parent's involved, too."

Mrs. Guthrie looked at her daughter's stricken face. "You've really got theater in your blood now, haven't you? Sure, I guess we can both go and try out for parts as wedding guests. That shouldn't be too bad. Then Viola Nolton can have a clearer shot at being the love interest, and her mother can stop making snide comments about me."

By the time Sid got herself and her mother to the theater, she was a nervous wreck. She had offered to carry the Xeroxed scripts, and just before leaving had managed to substitute the special pages she and Joel had typed before Xeroxing, careful revisions of the originals.

Now she looked nervously around the crowd that milled about the auditorium. She didn't see Rev. Aikens yet, but Joel was slumped down in an aisle seat. Joining him, she flopped the heavy bag of scripts beside her. He looked as pale as she felt.

Suddenly Mrs. Nolton came bustling down the aisle like a purposeful chicken. Sid jumped up and handed her the scripts, sure that those few extra pages stood out like neon. But the woman only thanked her absently and, hurrying onto the stage, placed some of the scripts on a waiting table.

More people came in. The director finished talking with the wardrobe mistress, and sat down in the second row. "All right, all women who want to try out for wedding guests, please go up onstage."

Suddenly Sid was twice as nervous, for herself this time.

She didn't really care about being a wedding guest. But she *had* to be onstage at the right time.

Seven women walked up onto the stage. Sid noticed Mrs. Nolton's relieved smile when her mother went up. Viola was one step closer to the part of the bride.

"Now ladies," the director announced, "each one take a script off that table and get into some sort of line."

To Sid's horror, she found herself at one end of the line. She prayed it was the far end. Her throat was dry, and her hands were so sweaty, she was afraid she'd spot the script.

"You on the end, Miss Guthrie, turn to page six and seven. Read all the women's parts; I'll feed you the lines between."

Sid stepped forward. Like a firing line, she thought. The script shook in her hand. Her first line, "Right nice wedding," came out as a squeak.

But the second one, "Oysters for supper," struck her as funny, and she got more into the spirit of things. By the time she got to "Henry, Henry, you've been drinking cider!" she was belting them out as she imagined guests at a quaint country wedding might.

Before she realized it, she was through. Her mother, next in line, went through the same dialogue, and was followed by the other women. Then they were told to sit down while the director made some notes. Finally she announced that they'd all be guests except two (who'd been pretty poor), who would be jurors.

Next came tryouts for the female lead. It was between Viola Nolton and Alice Fitz, wife of a bank clerk. Viola won hands down. It was definitely a young buxom part.

By this time in tryouts, Sid could normally relax. But the minister still hadn't shown up. Sid felt like a juggler with too many balls in the air. Standing up, she paced around like a cat.

"Now," the director announced, "will all the men

interested in the parts of Jabez Stone, Daniel Webster, or the Devil, please get up onstage."

To Sid's enormous relief, Dennis Aikens burst through the door and hurried down the aisle. After greeting several people, he stopped by Sid.

"Sorry I'm late. Had to visit someone in the hospital. Have I missed things completely?"

"No, you're just in time. You're supposed to be up onstage right now." He turned a little pale, but hustled off to join the others.

"Mr. Scratch first, please."

Two men walked over to the script table. Sid recognized Dr. Styles, her dentist, and Paul Klein, a clerk at the five-and-dime. The dentist, she was sure, had it made. He'd always struck her as devilish, bending over her with a screeching drill. Wild bushy eyebrows, black hair slicked back.

After they both read one of Scratch's speeches, the clerk also tried out for Daniel Webster. He was pretty good, if a bit flowery, and Sid was worried. Suppose he got it and not Rev. Aikens?

Beside her, Joel clearly shared her doubts. "Maybe we could drug his tea so Aikens has to stand in for him."

But they needn't have worried. The minister looked ill-at-ease standing onstage, but as soon as he began Webster's speech, something grand seemed to take over. In a voice rolling like summer thunder, he spoke of freedom and justice and the simple joys of living. With one hand upraised and the other clutching the script, his voice rose in ringing conclusion. "All, all have played a part. It may not be denied in Hell, nor shall Hell prevail against it!"

The sparse audience broke into applause. While they all took a short break, Sid ran backstage to congratulate him. The young minister looked shy and uncomfortable again.

"You don't sound like that on Sundays," she said, awkwardly shaking his hand.

"No, I know. But my dad was a real old-timer preacher. Some of that rubbed off, I guess."

People settled down to hear the next tryout, for the part of Jabez Stone. The clerk had decided not to bother competing against Byron Vincenti—not for a part that demanded romantic good looks. Maybe he could still get the role of the fiddler or the judge.

The director was sitting back in her seat. "Anyone else want to try out for the part of Jabez? No? Well, okay Byron, for form's sake why don't you read us the long speech starting on page ninteen. Mary has just said, 'Oh, Jabez, why didn't you tell me?'"

Sid watched Byron, in voice, face, and posture, seemed to become Jabez Stone—a big capable farmer with country calm laid over great tension and fear. Slowly in everyday words, he told his new bride how seven years earlier he had sold his soul to the Devil. Byron wasn't using the script, he knew the part already. He turned, and seemed to look shame-faced at his young bride. Slowly he continued.

"Well, that's all there is to it, I guess. He came along the next afternoon, that fellow from Boston—and the dog looked at him and ran away. I had to make it more than two cents, but he was agreeable to that. So I pricked my thumb with a pin and signed the paper. It felt hot when you touched it, that paper, I keep remembering that."

He paused, looked away, then continued, his voice slowly rising in intensity. "And it all came true; he kept his part of the bargain. I got the riches, and I've married you. And—oh God Almighty, what shall I do?"

The words rang out in a spellbound, silent theater. Silent as death. Silent except for shadows whispering like rustling curtains at the back of the theater.

Several months passed. Spring misted the hills in delicate young green with here and there a pale drift of blossoming dogwood or a flamboyant splash of redbud. In town, the grass was growing again, already looking shaggy, like hair in need of a barber. But no one could bear to cut it yet—because of the violets and the profusion of dandelions. Even their fresh golden sunbursts were welcome after the winter.

A further very local sign of spring was the activity at the Blake Theater, which was well into preparation of its spring show.

During this month of rehearsal, Sid had forced herself to pay attention to her schoolwork so her grades didn't too clearly reflect her absorption with theater and with souls and with a mad scheme for bringing the two together. All she didn't need now was to have her teachers or mother decide that theater was a bad influence on her.

Now, however, as she ate lunch in the school cafeteria, she was definitely thinking about it all. Today she sat alone. Becky was out with a cold, and for days Susan Bron and Ella Lawrence had been in a contest over who could act the most outrageously dreamy over their current boyfriends. Sid wasn't in the mood for that today.

Suddenly a figure was standing over her. She looked up. Joel smiled and folded his tall frame into the chair across from her.

"At least school cooking is consistent," he said, sliding his tray onto the table. "Their pizza's always the same: cardboard spread with old liver."

Sid had scarcely touched her own piece of pizza and was working on her canned peaches. "Tell me, from your perch up in the light booth, how does the show seem to be coming?"

"Pretty good. Maybe we ought to go into playwriting. Nobody's noticed those lines we rewrote."

She nodded. "But if you think about them, they do seem a little out of place. I mean, why would Webster suddenly break into Latin like that? But the whole play's so weird anyway, I guess no one would notice."

Joel scraped the topping off his pizza and started eating the crust. "Right. I still don't know if I like how they're doing the jury of the dead, all done up like mimes in black and white. I'm not sure if it's effective or just screwy."

"I bet the audience will like it."

"Oh they'll probably think it's very artsy and avant-garde, or think they're *supposed* to think that."

"Well, it does give you a chance to do some wild stuff with lights."

Joel nodded and dipped his peanut butter cookie in the juice from the peaches. "That scene and the one where the Devil opens his box. This is a fun show for the light crew."

"It might be even more fun on the last night. Oh, I wish we didn't have to wait so long to try this."

"Me too," Joel agreed. "But we don't really know what will happen. We could end up completely wrecking the show."

"Or just as likely nothing at all will happen. That stuff we put together is a real hodgepodge. There's nothing exactly like it in the book."

"Necessity is the mother of invention. Good thing the props lady agreed to substitute real candles for the electric ones—after I sabotaged them anyway. You got the extra lines memorized?"

"Yes, but I'm not sure of my Latin pronunciation." She drank down the last of her milk. "But at least we have a real minister. Dennis has turned out to be pretty good, hasn't he?"

"He has. You deserve awards for recruiting him, no matter how the rest goes."

She tipped her head as if acknowledging the praise of multitudes. Then lowering her voice she said, "But have you noticed how Byron's been acting lately?"

"Yeah, and so has everybody else. They think he's on the verge of a nervous breakdown. His acting is still terrific but they've never seen him get so completely into a role, or have so hard a time getting out of it. Poor guy, I guess this one's just a little too close to home."

Sid covered the ghastly remains of her pizza with a greasy napkin. "I know. It must be awful for him. And that's not the only thing people have been noticing. Those cast-off spirit things have been acting up lately and more people have been catching glimpses of them. Pretty soon word's going to get around that the Blake Theater is definitely haunted."

"Should do wonders for business," he said dryly.

"Not when people learn it's true."

Joel glanced at the cafeteria clock. "Time to bid farewell to this enticing lunch tray."

Standing up, Sid was just composing a witty reply, when she saw Viola Nolton threading her way through the lunch tables toward them.

"I'm glad I caught you two *together*," she said with a cloying smile. "My mother said to give you these." She handed them two booklets.

Sid stared at the green paper cover. The black printing seemed to jump out at her like an accusation. "*The Devil and Daniel Webster:* play in one act; by Stephen Vincent Benét."

"These just came in," Viola informed them. "The play service must have realized their mistake and *finally* sent us the right ones. Mother says these are more convenient than the Xeroxed scripts, so we're to switch over."

As she watched Viola's retreating back, Sid wasn't even sure she'd gotten out a mechanical "thank you." All she knew was that their careful plans were tumbling down around them like shacks in an earthquake.

CHAPTER

11

Two days later, the sky was as gray and gloomy as their mood. Sid and Joel had arranged to meet after school at the main door. By unspoken consent, they drifted across the parking lot toward the elementary school playground. No point in exposing themselves to either comments or interruptions.

At last night's rehearsal, their fears had been realized. The changes they'd made on pages sixteen and seventeen had been noticed. No one had been blamed. The assumption was that the changes had been made years earlier to the script Mrs. Guthrie had copied, perhaps by some frustrated Latin scholar.

But as Sid had whispered to Joel, it wasn't the blame she cared about, but the effect. And the effect was that the director had decided to return to the official version. In terms of the internal logic of the play, that made sense. In terms of their plans to help Byron Vincenti, it was devastating.

Now Sid slouched against the cold metal pole of a swing set. "So what do we do next?"

Kicking at the hollowed-out sand under the swings, Joel said, "Nothing, I expect. What can we do?"

"Do you think maybe if we talked to Dennis and

explained . . ? I mean, now that he's gotten to know Byron, maybe he'd be willing to say those lines anyway. That's all we really need."

Absently, Joel grabbed hold of a chain and hoisted himself standing into the swing, both big feet jammed into the canvas sling. "I don't know, Sid. Think about it. I mean, he's a nice guy, but he *is* an adult. Is he going to believe any of this?"

Sid sighed and watched the wind scud a candy wrapper across the playground. "No, probably not. Guess we're back where we started. Not only is Dennis an adult, he's a very up-to-date type minister. I don't think they teach them much anymore about ghosts or witches or devils. I mean, that's very fine in most cases, but . . . ."

"But not when you're dealing with ghosts or witches or devils."

"Right." She sighed again. The candy wrapper had foundered in a rain puddle. "I just wish there were something we could do to help Byron. I've almost gotten to like him—I mean, now that I know why he's so weird. And he's been sort of friendly to me lately—I guess he doesn't have to hide anything now. You can't help but feel sorry for him—all those years afraid to stay in one place or make friends."

Pushing off with one foot, Joel swung meditatively back and forth. "Yeah, if he could ever get himself back together, he might be an okay sort of guy."

Sid kicked at the pole, making a dull metallic gonging. "Blast those play service people! When will we ever get another chance like that?"

"Never, probably," Joel said gloomily as he jumped down into the rain-dampened sand. "But we can keep our eyes open. Maybe something will turn up."

But nothing did. Rehearsals relentlessly ran into dress

week, and the play finally opened. Sid never remembered being so down for an opening night.

The play went well, nonetheless. The audience and critics seemed to love it. And true to Sid's predictions, great numbers of ladies from the church came backstage afterward to compliment and gush over their minister. Sid was glad the whole thing hadn't been a total waste. Dennis Aikens did seem to be enjoying himself. If only . . .

But after a couple of performances, Sid refused to brood anymore. It wouldn't have worked anyway, she decided. All that stuff in the book was probably just a lot of made up hocus-pocus. It was silly to have taken it seriously.

Although no longer so disappointed, Sid found the second weekend of the show went no better for her. On Saturday, she missed the cue for her one line, and someone had to ask in a loud voice, "I wonder what's for supper?" before she remembered to grab up her china platter with its gray Styrofoam chunks and shout "Oysters for supper!"

Then at the end, when they all mobbed around the Devil and beat him with brooms and flails, Dr. Styles accidentally stomped on her foot and someone swatted her in the face with a broom.

The curtain call proved far worse. Ranged in a long line, the wedding guests and jurymen were to trot out and take the first bow. Then they were to step back altogether and let the principals through for their bow.

After the curtain opened, Sid stepped forward on cue. As directed, she was clutching the blue-and-white china platter with the phony oysters. She bowed, but failed to step back as soon as the others. Suddenly seeing she was alone, she scurried backward and collided with Viola, who was striding forward to take her bow.

The platter jolted forward, spraying its Styrofoam oysters down into the orchestra pit. The audience broke into laughs, and Viola shot her a furious glare for having stolen the attention.

As far as Sid was concerned, once she was offstage she couldn't get changed and headed home fast enough. But the props mistress tracked her down at the makeup tables.

"Sidonie, dear, I don't mean to be a bother, but do you think after you've changed you could go into the pit and pick up those oysters. I've made arrangements for after the show, and . . ."

"And it was my fault. Sure, Mrs. Hills, I'll pick them up."

"Well, that is nice of you. But I wouldn't call it your fault entirely. Viola does always seem to be in a rush to get her applause."

Once she was back in jeans and sweatshirt, Sid trudged down the side stairs into the orchestra pit. She could see gray oysters scattered over the whole space. If only they hadn't been storing things in the pit during this nonmusical show! She'd never find all the little chunks of Styrofoam with all these curtains and backdrops everywhere.

Feeling very much put upon, she sighed and began picking up oysters and dropping them into a heap on one of the old curtains. Maybe if she pretended she were looking for Easter eggs . . .

"Oysters for supper?" came a voice from behind her.

She spun around and threw a featherweight oyster at Joel's grinning face. "Just you hush!"

"Now be nice, and maybe I'll help. Then after the seafood is taken care of, can you stay and talk? I've been thinking about . . . our little problem."

Sid nodded. After they'd assembled a reasonable number of oysters, she hurried up to the props table for the platter. Her mother was just walking by.

"Oh, there you are, Sidonie. You ready to go yet?"

"Eh . . . not quite, Mom. I've got to stay and pick up all those blasted oysters. But you don't have to wait."

"I don't want you walking home alone."

"I know. But . . . but Joel's helping me with the oysters. Maybe he'll walk me home."

Her mother gave her a quick wistful smile. "Oh, that's fine, then. I'll leave some cocoa on the stove."

By the time Sid returned to the orchestra pit with the platter, most of the other people had left the theater. Joel was sitting comfortably on a stack of old curtains.

Sid plunked the platter down beside the heaped oysters and began scooping them in. "So what have you been thinking?"

"Well, it seems to me there might be another approach. First we tried tricking a minister into saying the appropriate words. You say we'll never convince him to do it voluntarily; and you're probably right, he'd never taken our word for all this. But suppose Byron himself went and asked him for help? A minister couldn't turn down a plea like that, could he?"

"Well, no, I guess not. But suppose Byron can't stand churches and crosses? You know, like Dracula."

"Ah, that's because vampires are evil. But Byron's not evil. He can't be, can he? Without a soul, I mean."

"Hmm. Yes, maybe it is a good idea. But would Byron do it? I mean, if he'd wanted to take his problem to a minister, wouldn't he have done it by now? After all, he's had enough time."

Joel sighed and kicked a heel against the stacked curtains. "Yeah, you're probably right. Byron does seem the stubborn, go-it-alone type. But I wonder if there isn't some way we can get him to try it. I mean, maybe he's just given up fighting, and stopped trying new angles."

"He did take a try at witchcraft to get rid of those ghost things."

"Right, he did," Joel agreed dejectedly. "Well, let's just think a minute. There ought to be something we can come up with."

By now, the last of the cast and crew had left. The theater was quiet and dark except for light filtering in from the hallway. Sid was happy enough to spend some time thinking about their dilemma, but she wished they could do it somewhere else.

At least, she thought, Byron had stopped hanging around the theater after the show. Probably he'd had enough of his ghostly shadows. But then, so had she.

"Joel," she whispered, "how about our going now and talking about this on the way home?"

He didn't answer for a moment.

"Joel," she began again.

"Shh. Did you hear something?"

The hair prickled along her arms. She *had* heard something. Sort of a faint swishing from up onstage.

More bravely than she felt, she whispered, "It's just those things again."

"Maybe. But there was something else—footsteps."

She listened. From way upstage, she did hear footsteps. Several steps, a pause, then several more. Could it be Byron? Mellowed or not, she didn't want another run-in with him here.

She'd opened her mouth to urge that they leave, when she heard another sound. It quavered on the edge of hearing. Then slowly it lowered into a scream. She had heard it before—the screamer with the sword.

The scream went on and on. Suddenly it was cut into by a voice from onstage. "No! Go away!" Footsteps. Hurried footsteps, coming closer. Closer to where they huddled below in the orchestra pit.

For a second, a dark shape loomed above them on the

101

edge of the stage. A startled gasp. The figure swayed, then toppled down toward them.

Something heavy smacked Sid across the face. Somebody's arm? A flesh-and-blood person groaned, sprawling between the two of them on the pile of old curtains. The person disentangled itself from them and struggled to sit up.

"Who are you?" a man's voice quavered in the semi-darkness.

"Sidonie Guthrie."

"Joel Griggins."

"Thank God. It's me, Dennis Aikens. Did . . . did you see that thing?"

"Not tonight," Sid said. "We have before, though. But don't worry, it won't hurt us. It's just an act."

Sid felt the man beside her shudder. "Ghosts! I really didn't believe I'd see them. Surely nothing like that."

"Did you come here looking for ghosts?" Joel asked, surprised.

"Well, I suppose I did. But I didn't expect to find them. You see . . . Are you sure it's safe down here?"

"Perfectly. But go on."

"Well, Dahlia Nolton came to my office yesterday. I was a bit surprised since she's not a parishioner. But she said she had a problem, and I was the only one she could think to turn to. Ah, the snares of flattery!

"With a perfectly straight face, she told me that she and Viola had seen ghosts in this theater, and that others had seen them too. That sounded pretty ridiculous, but Mrs. Nolton is not the sort of person you make light of—not to her face. And anyway, I suddenly remembered those comments about the haunted theater in Rev. Farley's old journal. So I told her I'd check it out, though I don't know what she expected of me—some sort of Hollywood exorcism maybe."

"Or," Joel suggested, "maybe she thinks all ministers keep ghostbuster backpacks in their closets."

"Right, along with the vestments." Dennis laughed nervously. "But now I'm beginning to think that wouldn't be such a bad idea. Sidonie, you said you've seen that . . . that thing before?"

"Yes several times. That one and some of the others."

"Others?" The voice tightened with alarm.

Sid, however, was paying more attention to Joel, who was jabbing her meaningfully in the ribs.

"Well, sir," he said, barely suppressing the excitement in his voice, "it all stems from a problem we thought you could help us solve, but we haven't known how to tell you about it. We were afraid you'd find it pretty unbelievable."

The minister sighed and shifted his position so that his knees were drawn up to his chin. "Well, run it past me now. This seems to be my day for the unbelievable."

For twenty minutes, they explained what they knew about the theater "ghosts" and their unfortunate author. They also outlined their thwarted plans to help him. They were interrupted only once—by the sad silent drifting of a figure in Puritan black through the empty air above the orchestra pit.

For a time after they'd finished their narrative, Dennis said nothing. Then he laughed quietly. "Let me spell this out slowly. As a result of all this, you want me to be part of some archaic ceremony for reclaiming mortgaged souls, and you want me to do it onstage?"

"Well, we figured that was the only way to set it up," Sid explained. "Byron would be on hand, we could arrange all the paraphernalia and drawings, and a real minister could say the proper words. And still, if it didn't work, nobody would be likely to guess anything special was going on."

"Yes, I see that. But now that I know about it, wouldn't it

be better just to ask Byron to drop by my office sometime and try it there?"

Joel cleared his throat uncomfortably. "Well, sir, maybe you're right, but we sort of thought that Byron in his present . . . condition, maybe wouldn't feel too comfortable in churches."

"Hmm, yes. That could explain why he thought it so hysterically funny when I suggested he add his fine baritone voice to our church choir."

He was silent a moment, then continued. "Well, assuming everything is exactly as you said—and I'm not conceding that yet, but assuming it is—then the appropriate thing might be to follow your plan. But even so, I don't think I'm the sort of person you need for it. After all, I hardly . . ."

"But, Dennis," Sid interrupted with wheedling innocence. "Isn't it every minister's job to save lost souls?"

He groaned. "Well and truly snared. Look, give me a night and a day to wrestle with all this. Then why don't you both come by my office after school on Monday? And Sid, you bring that wretched book. Then we can either have a therapy session or a council of war."

He stood up, keeping slightly bent over for fear of another swooping wraith.

"My father would certainly be proud of me now. He viewed every Sunday sermon as a chance to do battle with the Devil." Dennis laughed ruefully. "But I hate to think what my instructors at the seminary would say."

CHAPTER 12

It was late afternoon on a fine spring Saturday. Not a mild day, but a vigorous one. A jaunty wind beat at the trees and their young green leaves. The very air seemed vital, sparkling with energy and promise.

As Sid walked to the theater, she tried to take in every detail of the scene. She wanted to get her mind off what she was about to do and lock into it a picture of the bright real world. For all she knew, they'd be descending into the depths of Hell tonight, or at least poking around in the outskirts.

She'd told her mother that Joel had asked her to come early and help with some of the lighting and special effects. Her mother gave her one of those maddening smiles, which Sid supposed should have annoyed her more than it did. Relunctantly, Sid had concluded that if it was all right for her to keep tabs on her mother's male companions, she shouldn't object if her mother did the same with her. Besides, her mother was off base; Joel was just a good friend.

Once at the theater, Sid found Joel on his hands and knees near the center of the stage. The large leather-bound book was open in front of him, and with one hand he was carefully chalking a five-sided figure on the worn boards.

The tip of his tongue stuck out as he concentrated on drawing each line exactly right.

They were alone in the theater, but even so, Sid whispered. "Be sure you get all those lines closed. They made a big deal about that in the book."

"I will, I will. But it probably doesn't matter too much as long as we conjure up what we're supposed to. I mean, surely one loose soul couldn't cause too much damage—even an actor's soul. Still . . . . if we *have* done something wrong, there's always the danger of having a demon with big fangs hopping about the place." He made a monster face at Sid, and she swatted him over the head with a rolled up script.

"Well, we haven't! And anyway, we've got an ordained minister on hand to deal with anything of that sort."

Joel stood up, dusting off the knees of his jeans. "Don't know if I'd count on that too much. From what Dennis said, I don't think they offer Demonology 1A in seminaries anymore, at least not in the one he went to."

Sid decided not to think about the unfunny side of that remark. Reaching into her pocket, she threw Joel a roll of silver duct tape. "Here, master artist, cover those lines so they don't get scuffed away during the show."

Joel returned to hands and knees and carefully taped over the lines. "In stagelight, nobody ought to notice this stuff, not with the other scraps of tape still here from marking where furniture went in other shows. Someday they really ought to refinish this whole stage."

While he worked, Sid reached into her other pocket and pulled out two black candles. Walking to the sideboard, she removed a white candle from a pewter candlestick and replaced it with a black one.

"You have no idea how hard it is to find *black* candles," she complained. "I finally got someone at the five-and-dime to root around in their storeroom. They found this with the Halloween stuff."

"Good, good. I'm glad Dennis noticed it specified black candles. In fact, I'm glad Dennis checked over the whole thing, though he keeps saying it's not his field."

Sid nodded. "He still seems pretty unsure about this, though I guess now it's caught his professional interest."

Joel glanced up as Sid walked across to the table and replaced the other candle. "Make sure that one's lined up with this point of the pentangle. Then one point will line up with where Byron will stand, two with the candles, one with your spot, and the other with where I'll be in the wings. Then when Dr. Styles steps into the center of the pentangle with Scratch's soul box and Dennis moves to that spot I've chalked here, everything ought to move like clockwork."

"Knock on wood," Sid cautioned. "Tim didn't mind your taking his place by the sound effects table tonight?"

"No, he's been after me to let him to do lights on his own for the last two shows. He's good; he can handle it. And I can do the bell and thunder and all the scripted sound effects, all right. And I'm sure I can do as spooky a lost soul's voice as Tim. I'm just not sure about the unscripted stuff, my Latin pronunciation's not too good."

"Mine neither. But we're just supporting cast. Besides, no one's supposed to hear us but the Cosmos or something."

They heard voices in the hall. The more punctual crew and cast members were arriving for the 6:30 call. "I'd better go get ready," Sid said, hurrying off. Then she turned back and smiled tautly at Joel. "Break a leg."

As she walked toward the dressing rooms, Sid wondered if being in the hospital with a broken leg might not be preferable tonight. Her mind was so occupied as she pulled on her costume that it wasn't until she tried lacing it up that she realized she had the long gingham dress on backward.

Annoyed, she shifted it around then headed for the makeup tables.

Staring at the mirror, she wondered if her terror was as plain to others as it was to her. Disguise time, she thought, and liberally plastered on base and rouge. Her hand shook so badly while she was applying the eyeliner, she had to smear it off and try again.

Her mother, wearing a similar farm wife's costume, came in and looking her daughter over, sat down beside her.

"Nervous tonight, honey?"

Annoyed at herself for being so transparent, Sid only nodded. If she was really going to be an actress, she'd have to do better than this.

"Well, that's natural," her mother continued as she unscrewed the top of a jar. "The last night and all. Everyone's up for it." She lowered her voice. "Byron's so tense, he almost snapped my head off when I said hello to him. Poor guy, I just wish he would ease up a little. He seems even worse with this show. I almost feel sorry for Viola playing opposite him, ninny though she may be."

Others in the cast were drifting in to put on their makeup. Mrs. Guthrie looked up from applying base to the back of her hands, and smiled. Sid followed her gaze to see Dennis Aikens walking in. In his frock coat and top hat he was quaint and jaunty looking. But Sid also noticed an unusually pale, tight look on his face. He too needs to work on his offstage acting, she thought.

But she could see him making the effort as he plunked himself down on a nearby stool. He scowled at the mirror, then sighed deeply, "It's no use!" he complained to the world in general. "I can handle the base and, God help me, the lipstick. But I can't do the eye makeup. I look like Frankenstein's monster after a night on the town. Somebody help!"

He would have had no shortage of helpers; Dennis was

108

already a well-liked member of the company. But Mrs. Guthrie got there first. Sid discreetly slipped away. This had possibilities.

Sid walked out into the corridor and with forced casualness leaned against a wall near the props table, waiting for her next secret cue. After a while she found she'd twisted the ribbon on the front of her dress into knots.

At the far end of the corridor, she could see Byron Vincenti pacing back and forth. Tension almost crackled around him like lightning. And when he glanced her way, an inner agony seemed chiseled into his face. Fear and pity surged up within her. She was glad he knew nothing about their plans. She couldn't bear it if he had to watch them fail.

She jumped as a hand dropped onto her shoulder. Dennis. His eyes were made up perfectly, and a wan smile fluttered under his mustache.

"Ready to do battle?"

"As ready as I'll ever be."

His eyes shifted toward the dark figure pacing at the end of the corridor. "I'm hopelessly torn between wanting this to work and hoping that nothing whatsoever happens."

"Yeah, I know."

"There's one other problem. If I come out with those weird lines and nothing does happen, I'm going to look like a gibbering idiot."

"Not really. You can just say afterward that in the heat of the moment, your mind slipped back to the lines we rehearsed at first."

"Yes, there's that out." He lowered his voice even further. "I suppose what I'm really afraid of is finding that there *is* something to all this."

"Places in five minutes!" the stage manager suddenly announced behind them. They both jumped, then looked at each other and laughed.

Patting her arm, Dennis drifted off to join some of the

others, and Sid resolutely walked over to the props table where, as usual, Martha Hills was fumbling with last-minute problems.

"Would you like me to go out and light the candles for you, Mrs. Hills?" Sid asked.

"Oh yes, Sidonie, dear, that would be a big help. I can't seem to find that little purse Second Man is supposed to have. There are the matches, dear."

Taking the book of matches, Sid hurried out onto the stage. Tonight, she didn't want anyone moving those candles, even fractionally, or worse, making a last-minute switch back to the white ones.

Sid hated lighting matches. She struck one so many times, the cardboard stick crumpled hopelessly. The next one lit on the third try. When she'd finally gotten the second candle going, she looked into the wings where the sound effects table stood. Joel wasn't there. A moment's panic. But he must be up in the light booth giving Tim last-minute instructions. She prayed he'd get down in time. Surely, he would; if anyone here was a theater professional, Joel was.

"Places everybody! Curtain in five minutes."

Sid scurried off to drop the matches back on the props table, then joined the others as they walked quietly to their places.

Mechanically, Sid took up her spot by the fireplace where she was supposed to be when the curtain opened, holding her platter of oysters and gossiping with Mildred Pearsons, who played First Woman. She smiled nervously at Mildred and tried to imagine that this was just a regular performance.

She picked up the platter from the hearth and thought about her line, her one line. Some immortality! Maybe Byron had brought this thing on himself, but she could certainly feel for him. Someone with talent, who loved the stage, always getting bit parts—that could drive a person to doing something horrible, something like . . .

Stop it! she told herself. Think about . . . oysters. She looked at the little chunks of Styrofoam. Their gray paint was thick and shiny, making them look like melted marshmallows from some old pharoah's tomb. How could anyone believe they were oysters, even from a distance? They certainly hadn't fallen like oysters. She remembered watching them through an embarrassed haze as they drifted like snow into the orchestra pit.

And it was a good thing they had, come to think of it, or Dennis would never, quite literally, have fallen in with their scheme. She was glad he was part of it now, though having an adult involved didn't make her nearly as confident as she would have thought. Even though he'd gone over that book and others again and again, Dennis still seemed unsure about what this would do. Probably, she suspected, a big fat nothing. But still, suppose it was like one of those movies where stupid people are always "tampering with things best left unknown"? Suppose they conjured up things with claws and . . .

Stop it! Think of . . . nothing.

She tried to erase her mind: a blank sheet taking on impressions. Beyond the thick curtains, she could hear the audience, voices and people shifting about. It sounded like a pretty full house. She hoped this little plot of their didn't wreck the show for them. Good thing Becky wasn't coming again tonight. She hoped . . .

Stop it!

The audience quieted. Out beyond the curtains, the houselights must have dimmed. Suddenly she was afraid. She wanted to run out of the theater, out of town, and never come back. Frantically she looked into the wings. Hidden among the leg curtains, Joel stood by the sound effects table. Under his mop of pale hair, his face was even paler. But he smiled tensely and flashed her a thumbs-up sign.

"Open in five," the stage manager whispered. "Five, four, three, two, one."

With creaking and swooshing the curtain opened. The lights came up in an 1840s New England farmhouse, and over by the sideboard, Paul, the five-and-dime clerk, struck up the fiddle. Sid was concentrating so hard on thinking only about the show, she nearly missed her cue again.

"Handsome couple," observed First Man.

Startled, Sid walked quickly to the table and loudly proclaimed, "Oysters for supper!" What a dumb line. Well, she thought, at least she was back to normal. Just flow with the play for a bit.

The others went on with their lines. Already the battery of lights was super-heating the stage. Sid could feel the sweat beading on her forehead, but she dared not rub it away for fear of smearing the makeup.

The wedding guests went on celebrating, all the while gossiping about how Jabez Stone could have come by all his money.

"She's a lucky woman. They're a lucky pair."

"That's true as gospel. But I wonder how he got it?"

"Money, land, and riches."

"Just came out of nowhere."

"Wonder where he got it. But that's his business."

They danced and gossiped and drank pretend cider, and gradually worked to the back of the set so Jabez and Mary could have their scene.

The curtained window Sid stood by looked out on a sheet of plywood, lit now by the rose of sunset. But instead of gazing out, she turned slightly to watch Byron and Viola do their scene. Even in his quite ordinary lines, Byron was riveting. Viola looked sweet and buxom in her billowy white dress, but occasionally her lines were lost under the howling of the wind outside. That was never true of Byron's. Even when whispering, his voice reached to the high rafters.

Then Daniel Webster made his entrance, and the guests rushed forward again. Dennis no longer looked like a scared, doubt-stricken young minister, but a cocky, big-name politician getting into the mood of a country wedding. Sid felt a surge of pride and affection toward the man, and turned it into enthusiastic cheering for Webster.

Suddenly the fiddler struck a discordant note, and in walked Mr. Scratch, a metal insect-collecting box under his arm. Sid started. She wished things weren't going so fast. It was almost time.

Scratch, dressed jarringly in red and black, began chatting with the other wedding guests, slowly moving toward Jabez and Webster. Sid couldn't bear to watch Byron, his horror looked so real. She kept her eyes on Dr. Styles. A very good job of makeup, very devilish. She wondered if she could ever allow him to work on her teeth again.

The fiddler screeched a second time. Annoyed, Scratch put down his box and snatched away the fiddle. Playing an eerie discordant tune, he began circling around the newly-weds. The tension rose and rose until Mary shrieked and Webster yelled, "Stop, stop, you miserable wretch!"

Sid's secret cue. Under her breath she began chanting, *"In nomine Dei, in nomine Diaboli, perditam educe animam."*

Standing nearby, First Woman gave her a hushing look.

Sid took a couple of measured steps downstage, closed her eyes and continued chanting, *"In nomine Dei, in nomine Diaboli, perditam educe animam."* Joel, she knew, would be in position doing the same. She was sure they couldn't be heard from the audience, not with Webster and

Scratch shouting like that. Sid opened her eyes. Here it comes.

On cue, Scratch turned and saw the fiddler tampering with his collection box. "Idiot!" he shouted and rushed stage right, chasing the fiddler around the table. Scratch lunged. They wrestled for the box. The Devil stepped back, just as always, but now it was into the newly chalked pentangle.

The lights blacked out as usual, but suddenly nothing else was right, not right with the play, not right with their plan. The clap of thunder was not from Joel wiggling the sheet of metal backstage. It was huge and deafening and seemed to rise through the soles of their feet.

Under it, Sid heard a grunt and a thud, and as the lights rose, she glimpsed something hidden from the audience. Someone lay stunned under the table. It looked like Dr. Styles.

Instantly she looked up and nearly screamed. A figure stood in the pentangle. Same costume and makeup. But it radiated an intense imposing evil. This was no southern Indiana dentist.

Something began to rise from the box in the figure's hand. It was not the spotlight they used for the escaping soul scene. It had its own light, rising like glowing mist.

"Help me neighbors, help me!" A thin ghostly voice filled the hall. The right lines, but the wrong voice. It wasn't Joel's. Fearfully Sid glanced offstage. Joel stood by the table, his eyes wide, his mouth shut.

For a moment, everyone on stage was stunned. Something was clearly wrong. Suddenly pale despite his makeup, Dennis threw Sid a look filled with growing, terrified understanding. And suddenly she understood as well. They had called Byron's soul in the name of both God and the Devil, thinking that for an unclaimed denizen of limbo, that would help bring it forth. But it had also alerted, perhaps even summoned, the Devil. And now like the character he played, he held the soul, the real soul, in his hands.

Dennis turned away, struggling to fall back into character. Fumbling over the words, he finally got out Webster's line. "What's that? It wails like a lost soul."

"A lost soul," the wedding guests chanted. "Lost—lost in darkness."

"It sounds like Miser Stevens," the fiddler said a little weakly. It didn't sound anything like "Miser Stevens," and they all knew it.

For the first time anyone could remember, Byron Vincenti missed a cue. He stood like a horrified statue staring at "Mr. Scratch," who stared back, a death's-head grin on his face.

After a painful pause, the fiddler picked up the line. "Miser Stevens. But it can't be, he ain't dead."

"Miser Stevens, the soul of Miser Stevens. But he ain't dead."

Offstage, Joel jerked out of his trance and shakily rang the props bell.

"The bell!" the crowd intoned. "The passing bell. Miser Stevens—dead."

Mr. Scratch leered wickedly and reached up to snare the glowing thing in his red bandanna.

"Help me neighbors, help me!" Again the disembodied voice.

On cue, Webster stepped forward between Jabez and Scratch. His face had a look of grim determination they hadn't seen before. Pointing a finger toward the figure in red and black, he thundered out the old inserted lines. *"In nomine Dei, Ego in corpore animam revoco!* In the name of god, release that soul!"

Scratch only laughed. A horrible bone-tearing laugh that was nowhere in the script. He didn't say Scratch's next line.

He just stared insolently at Rev. Aikens, who firmly repeated his own line.

"In nomine Dei, Ego in corpore animam revoco," he shouted with new force. "In the name of God, release that soul!" The two characters stood as though alone on stage, their eyes locked in a battle of wills.

The scene around Sid shimmered in a haze of fear. They'd only meant to call up the soul of Byron Vincenti, not the Devil himself! And now Sid could see that Dennis was determined to fight for that soul, the soul they'd inadvertently put in the hands of the enemy. But for all that he was an ordained minister, Dennis was hopelessly outclassed here. He'd be fried to a cinder! And Sid knew it would be her fault.

Slowly Scratch crushed the writhing whiteness into his bandanna, and stuffed it back into the box.

Sweat broke out on Dennis's face. *"In nomine Dei, Ego in corpore animam revoco,"* he repeated hoarsely, his eyes never leaving his opponent.

The expression on Scratch's face tightened. With seeming difficulty he raised his hand and lowered the lid of the box. Then slowly, as though fighting against a great weight, he stretched a threatening hand toward the minister.

In guilt and anger, Sid screamed. Charging across the stage, she flung herself at the Scratch figure. Her shoulder burned as she smashed against him. The metal box flew from his grasp, and Sid rolled, dazed, to the floor.

Snarling, the figure lunged for the box, but collided with an unseen wall rising from the lines of the pentangle.

The box burst open at Jabez's feet.

All the lights went out. A soft white glow rose from the shattered box. Byron stared down into it, his features suffused with light and awe and growing joy. Exultantly he flung up his arms as the light faded into him.

In the darkness, a furious scream burst from where

Scratch had stood. The wild scream of a thwarted animal. It rolled on into a peal of thunder—thunder so powerful it shook the building.

The candle flames, the only lights onstage, suddenly flared, rising into two columns of fire. A jarring blast, like lightning. The flames wavered. In a cold gust of air, they snuffed out.

But not before two of the curtains had burst into flames.

"Fire!" someone yelled, and the awe was broken. The house lights came up, the panicky audience rushed for the doors, someone lowered the fire curtain, and onstage everybody was running about, getting in each other's way and looking for fire extinguishers.

Sid heard Joel's voice beside her, but it was a moment before she could understand his words. "It's all right. Are you hurt? It's over. Thank God, it's over."

As Joel helped her stand, Sid noticed Dennis Aikens helping a still groggy Dr. Styles out from under the table. They both looked pale and shaken, but the minister's face held a relieved understanding not shared by those around them.

Standing beside her, Joel touched Sid's shoulder. It was tender there, but the scorching pain was already fading. Smiling feebly, she looked up at him, then followed his gaze downstage. Where Byron Vincenti had stood, there was nothing but an empty metal box. At last he was free. Wherever he was, he was whole again. And she was happy for him.

CHAPTER

13

For weeks the main subject of talk around town was the strange show at the Blake Theater. The fire afterward had been put out without much damage except to the curtains. But that was minor compared to the rest.

In the end, the general conclusion was that the theater's temperamental star, Byron Vincenti, had finally cracked up, substituting some fellow nut for one of the actors and tampering with the lights and special effects. His disappearance afterward strengthened this view. Those who concluded differently, kept it to themselves.

Several weeks later, spring finally gave way to summer. The air was warm and damp, and the countryside smothered in lush green. In the evenings, fireflies twinkled among the trees. And finally, the last day of school came to an end.

Although he lived on the other side of town, Joel walked Sid home that afternoon. Sid might have objected once, she didn't now. They had gone through enough together that she didn't care who saw or said what.

As they opened the screen door and stepped into the relatively cool kitchen, they found Mrs. Guthrie and Rev. Aikens in friendly conversation at the kitchen table.

Sid's mother looked up and smiled. "Hi, kids. How went the last day of school?"

"As well as could be expected," Sid said, eyeing the plate of fresh butterscotch cookies on the table.

Dennis laughed. "Do have some. I suspect that your mother didn't make them entirely for me. We've just been talking about next year's shows."

Sid shot him a questioning look. "You mean, you're staying with the company?"

Dennis smiled at Sid and her mother. "Oh, the theater bug is hard to shake once it's bitten. Besides, this next season sounds a little more . . . manageable."

"It is a terrific season," Mrs. Guthrie said happily. *"A Midsummer Night's Dream, Iolanthe,* and *Peter Pan."*

"That does sound good." Sid lowered her eyes, afraid that if she looked at Dennis or Joel, she'd start laughing. "Now, about those cookies. How about our taking half."

Her mother chuckled. "Is that your final offer, or just a bargaining position? Sure, help yourself."

Sid quickly got a plate down from the cupboard and swept half the contents of the other plate onto hers. She and Joel took this booty, plus a couple of Cokes from the refrigerator, out onto the back porch. Fred, with some sixth sense about food, ambled around the corner of the house and settled himself hopefully at their feet.

For a minute, Sid and Joel sat in contented silence, munching cookies and letting the cool drink fight back some of the heat.

Finally Joel said, "You know, lately I had been thinking of taking up some less hazardous pastime—like motorcycle racing, maybe. But I've got to admit, that *does* sound like a good season."

"A little heavy on fairies, though," Sid said with a giggle. She selected another cookie and threw it to Fred.

"True, but not a witch, ghost or devil among them."

Sid laughed. "Good. And if six-inch-high fairies start

119

materializing, we should be able to . . . manage, like Dennis said."

Leaning back against a porch rail, she absently flicked a fingernail against loose chips of paint. "Doing *Peter Pan*, though, does sound exciting. Think of the flying." She hugged herself. "Oh, I'd give anything to get a part like Wendy."

Horror stricken, she clapped a hand to her mouth. Then jumping up, she shouted to the empty sky, "No! I retract the offer!"

She half expected the sky to darken and a howling wind to bring the scorching scent of sulfur. But the air remained soft and mild, carrying only the scent of honeysuckle and the distant calling of a dove. Stretched at their feet, Fred snoozed undisturbed in the sun.

She relaxed again, smiling sheepishly at Joel. He grinned back.

"From now on," he said, "the closest I want to get to anything supernatural is working the spotlight for the fairy effect."

Sid giggled. "And just think, instead of being in the program only as 'light crew' you can be listed with the cast as 'Tinker Bell.'"

He laughed with her. "Now *that* is immortality."

ABOUT THE AUTHOR

Growing up in California, Pamela F. Service developed interests in politics, history, and science fiction. She received a bachelor's degree from the University of California and a master's degree from the University of London. She has pursued her interest in history by touring ancient sites and digging in excavations in Britain and the Sudan.

Ms. Service currently lives in Bloomington, Indiana, with her husband and daughter where she is the curator of a local museum.